Jersey Flats

A Novel

RICHARD CURTIS HAUSCHILD

First published by Dog Ear Publishing
4010 W. 86th Street, Ste H
Indianapolis, IN 46268
www.dogearpublishing.net

ISBN: 978-160844-625-4

This book is printed on acid-free paper.

Printed in the United States of America

CHAPTER ONE

There is a place that I always meant to visit. By visit, I mean get out of the car and walk up to it. It is a rocky out-cropping, a bump in the middle of a prairie called Jersey Flats in the Kettle Moraine of Southeastern Wisconsin. Something is hidden there: something buried in the ground, beneath the boulders. I have reasoned that I might not actually ever find what it is, but when I finally stood there I would know what it was. Even with this alluring idea in my head, it took me years to follow up on it. In those years I lived much of my life in not so quiet desperation, looking under rocks for things like success, love, and happiness. You could refill a quarry with those rocks. I knew filling Roland's expectations would be even more difficult; I just didn't know that the quest would plant a mad look in my eye. I've caught it lately in the mirror. A flicker. No one knows it is there, but me. If the secret under my own surface is madness, the secret of Jersey Flats just may be hope.

There was a persistent easterly wind blowing down off The Ledge, filling the cracks of Ghost Farm with sneaky cold drafts. The gloom of gray flannel weather had gone on for almost two weeks and the month of March became a cursed thing; not so much muttered, but rather hissed. Molly Costello wondered how the sky could affect her so much. The gray-ness streak had shut down her writing and had given birth to a restlessness that kept pace with the wind. She had started to turn to the weather site on her computer each morning to look for relief, but the remorseless satellites only showed spinning, yet stagnant low pressure. The red 'L' became a symbol for another wasted day. The Scarlet Letter of another age.

At least her daughters, Melanie and Sonia, were pretty much self-sufficient on school mornings. That thought made her nod into her coffee mug as she sat in the writing studio that Roland Heinz had resurrected from an old cheese shed. She knew the girls would be up with an eye on the clock. The bus would be down on Highway 151 at 6:45 AM and the girls would not allow themselves to miss it. They were used to waking up knowing Mom would be in her studio. That was her job: Mom the writer. Sonia, who was born in the Sudan and adopted by Molly, was now already an 'old soul' of thirteen. She understood very well her mother's obsession. She did just okay in most of her school subjects, but excelled in creative writing. Molly often wondered how family genes could be absorbed by adoption, but they were with Sony. And Molly, the mother, always noted how pretty Sonia had become. Mel was always pretty, but Sonia had a slow growing beauty; a kind of radiation from the heart.

Melanie, also adopted by Molly, was born in Viet Nam. She was now seventeen and was going to finish high school a year early in two months and enroll in a special pre-med scholarship program at the University of Wisconsin in Madison. This was a path that concerned Molly, but Melanie's counselors had been persuasive. All in all, the girls were low maintenance kids; smart, kind, and adaptive. Lately Molly worried more about herself. It was the time in her life to do so.

As she pondered the futures of her daughters, there was an almost silent knock on the studio door. It was followed by the door opening a crack and Sonia whispering through the crack.

"Mom?"

"Come in, dear. You don't have to knock, you know."

Sonia came in with her smile shining across her brown face. "I thought maybe you were concentrating, Mom. You said you were having some writer's blockage and I didn't want to disturb you if the block was gone."

"That's very sweet, Sony. My block is somehow controlled by the weather. As soon as the sun comes back, I will get busy again."

"It's been gray for days."

"Yep, but it can't last forever," said Molly with a philosophical sigh. Sonia mimicked her mother's sigh almost

2

perfectly. "What else did you want, honey? Your bus is almost here."

"I wanted to remind you that I will be on the late bus today. Oh, and Melanie has a meeting after school and is getting a ride home from Heather's mom."

"Got it."

"And Mom..."

"Yes, Sonia?"

"Well, are you or aren't you going out with that guy that Pat knows? We were talking and..."

"You guys were talking about me dating? How boring."

"You should go."

"Maybe I will." Molly got up and walked over to Sonia and turned her around to the door. It was a not too subtle hint.

"You don't want to talk about it?"

"Not now. Maybe later."

"Pat says he's a nice guy, Mom."

"Pat says a lot of things. You'd better scoot."

"Okay, bye."

An instant later Molly was once again drumming her fingers on her computer keyboard. Nothing was coming. She closed the laptop and began to think about Pat Stirling's matchmaking. She decided to call her friend and see if she could ruin her morning coffee as revenge for using her daughters as tools of influence. Damn that Pat. Molly loved her, but she had already decided that the blind date would not happen. There was no answer at Pat's house when she called.

When days started like this, Molly often employed an old family remedy; one that Roland had taught her and the girls. After putting on a jacket and gloves, she went out into the yard and headed for the old yellow barn to visit with its wise inhabitant, the family owl.

The barn owl had served as a meditation mantra for Roland Heinz. The late great Roland Heinz was twice awarded the Pulitzer Prize for literature and, later in life, became Molly's adoptive father. When Roland had died five years ago, he had left his estate to his new daughter and her children in a gesture that had surprised the locals, to say the least. Molly had only known Roland for a little more than a week prior to her adoption by the famous author. Then the man had died. There was a subtle literary changing of the guard back then. Molly, who had been working for *Art Harvest* magazine and doing an interview of Roland, had suddenly become his posthumous protégé. Although the subsequent changes of address and lifestyle had gone seamlessly, following in Roland's deep footsteps had not followed suit.

Molly's switch from journalism to writing fiction did have a limited early success, however follow up had been slow and agonizing for her and her long time friend and publisher, Harry Stompe. After Roland's death, a long-missing manuscript by Roland had been discovered and bequeathed to Harry. It was a sensational read and, though difficult and complex, had sold like a classic. With the money, Harry had founded Stompe Publishing and Molly Costello had been his first client. Molly's first novel, *Silent Silos,* had been well received critically, but sales were poor. Her second novel, *Melting Earth,* had failed miserably on both counts. Molly's success arrow was now pointed decidedly downward. She had struggled to find a signature character to match Roland's popular Garnet Granger, the young morbidly obese girl, who searches the cosmos for love in dreams. Alas, it seemed there was only one Garnet in the cosmos.

As Molly's eyes adjusted to the darkness of the barn, she saw the three folding lawn chairs that had been there for owl observation since Roland had first showed the kids the way to watch the bird. It was sort of a family insider activity, which Roland had explained in his rather cosmic fashion; watching the owl was sharing the passage of time with Nature...or something like that. Molly didn't get it like Roland and the girls did. She came out to the barn to think. If the owl was there thinking along with her, well, that was fine. It was the atmosphere of almost cathedral-like quiet that appealed to Molly's sense of peace. The barn was lit by little holes in the roof that sometimes caused shafts of light to illuminate the dust motes into universes of floating objects. There were no such light shafts today since there was no sun. She sat down in the middle chair and looked for the owl. It was not where it usually was.

As Molly's eyes squinted upward to the rafters looking for the bird, she heard a rustling somewhere in a darkened corner. Her ears perked to the sound as it repeated itself. She got up slowly to investigate. God only knew what critter could be lurking in the shadows of the old barn. She followed the sound and quickly found the owl lying on the dirty floor, sporadically flapping its wings and spinning around on some strange axis. It was obviously in dire trouble.

When Molly touched it gently with the toe of her boot, the bird flipped over on its back and flailed at her boot with its talons. The effort was apparently exhausting as the owl quickly lost its defensive energy. Molly found her cell phone in her coat pocket and dialed Pat again. This time she answered.

"Good morning. Hey, Pat, do you know a veterinarian who does owls?"

CHAPTER TWO

After moving to the Midwestern countryside from New England, I found the wide open spaces to be somewhat daunting. That was before I began using them to my advantage. The ability to merely amble out my back door and walk for a long distance without having to deal with traffic or chat with nodding neighbors made more interesting journeys inside my head possible. I found that if something was bothering me, whether it is personal or literary, I would walk for a certain distance, say three miles, and pore over my problem. Then having defined it, I could walk the three miles back to the house while devising a solution. Combining mental health and physical health in one activity is a gift from the land I now own. A spirit is out there with me on my walks. Thank you, Roland. You truly are my father. I would miss you more, but your spirit here is so strong that it lives much like a sleeping dog, hidden under the bed.

Owen Palmer, DVM, was almost finished neutering his third black lab of the day. He was trying not to notice the adoring stares of his assistant, Jenny, as he performed the familiar task. He often thought if he never saw another black lab or golden retriever bound into his office in Long Lake, it would be too soon. The breeds were over employed in Wisconsin, not so much as hunting companions, but as cute puppies, which were in plentiful supply. Neutering and spaying at least was a small step in curtailing the chain of inbreeding and kennel over-population. It also kept his ledger black.

Jenny Fredericks was a very pretty young woman, blonde, slim, and all-season tanned, but she made Dr. Owen nervous. It was the unsteadiness of her perspective of him that caused this anxiety. Was she interested in him as a boss, a father figure, or a potential lover? There was a good twenty years divide in their ages, so perhaps the first two conjectures were more likely than the latter. And yet, there was definitely

adoration in those eyes. It was a daily work version of some sort of dating game. They were both single, nice looking, in close proximity, and both very unsure of what the next step should or could be. Neither knew whose court the ball was in, but then Fate usually takes care of overly careful people playing waiting games.

As he put the last stitch in a patient named Biff, the phone rang and Jenny ran to get it. Owen heard only bits and pieces of Jenny's end of the phone call as he washed up. He was hoping to get out of the clinic early today and had told her to take no new appointments. He knew by the look on her face when she came back that she had betrayed him.

"What is it, Jen?"

"You're going to hate me."

"Unlikely, but whatcha got?

"Well, a lady called, um, Ms. or Mrs. Costello, and she has a sick owl. I tried to tell her you were not seeing anyone today, but she said it was an emergency."

"An owl?"

"Yeah, Owen, a barn owl. Apparently, it is some family pet or something."

Own looked at his watch. "How soon?"

Jenny looked relieved that she hadn't messed his day. "She is on her way. She should be here in about a half hour."

"Where's she coming from?"

"Pipe."

Owen smiled and scratched his head. "A lady with a sick barn owl from Pipe." Fate also has a sense of humor it seemed. "But, Jen," Owen continued, "after her, nothing else, okay? I have to get out of here before noon."

Jenny smiled and nodded back at him; again adoringly, he thought. "Right-o," she said.

Owen had treated all sorts of wild creatures at his clinic in the tiny Kettle Moraine town of Long Lake, but never an owl. He went into his office and quickly found a veterinary web site that might have some tips for him. Within the site, he typed 'barn owl' into the search area. Soon he began to read all about *Tylo alba* and its common afflictions.

Dr. Owen Palmer was anxious to get away because he was meeting a group of local colleagues on a rare quest that afternoon. Something very unusual had happened in the area and he was going to be part of the investigation into a mystery. There was a sense of privacy and secrecy to the afternoon's activity, so he had not even mentioned it to Jenny. She was more than happy that they were closing up early. Now if this Costello woman and her sick owl would only show up. She was already late.

Despite Molly's sense of urgency regarding the owl, it had taken her some time just to get the bird captured and into a box for transportation to the vet. Once on the road she realized that she only had a vague idea where Long Lake was. She had to stop at the gas station in Waucousta and get directions. Even so, she missed a turn and was headed toward New Prospect before she realized she had missed County F. As she came to a stop sign at the intersection of County Roads SS and G, there was a large wooden sign that said she was at Jersey Flats. Then suddenly the sun, so long missing, came out with a startling brilliance through a hole in the clouds. She took that as a good sign and turned left to hopefully reconnect with the road to Long Lake. The owl was fluttering restlessly in the box, an old orange crate with a faded artwork label from Sarasota. Molly worried that it was hurting itself. As she drove north on County G, she saw the sun playing on the trees atop a little hill in the middle of the prairie. Something about it warmed her heart, but she also had a fleeting feeling that an exit portal to Heaven was opening for the owl. Twenty minutes later Molly found herself standing next to an examination table where Roland's owl was preparing to fly into the light.

"So that's it?" Molly asked, sad and exasperated at the same time. "There's nothing to do but let it die?"

Owen had not expected this drama while he waited for his last client of the day. "Folks bring in wild animals all the time, Ms. Costello. Sometimes if the problem is orthopedic I can fix it. Set a broken limb or something like that. But, a chronic affliction, which may in fact be simply old age, for a creature of the wild is a progression of Nature. There is no serum and no operation to perform on this bird. I am sorry."

Molly took a long, discerning look at the doctor for the first time. She had been so flustered when she arrived at the clinic that she could hardly take her eyes off the owl in its death throes. Dr. Palmer was nice looking she thought, in a country vet sort of way. She let her eyes roam the walls of his office, and she noted the various pictures that included the doctor with various smiling pet owners and pets. Okay, she thought, he is beloved. He is cute. He seems to be single (no ring). The age was close enough. So what is wrong with this man?

Owen had been looking at Molly similarly ever since she walked in, with much focus on the owl, too, of course. He recognized her face, but couldn't place her. It was to be a sincere opening for further conversation when suddenly the owl stopped moving. They both noticed at the same instant.

"Oh no!" Molly's eyes were searching Owen's face for something beside the obvious truth. He palpated the bird, looked up and shook his head.

"I'm sorry, but he is gone."

Molly could only shake her head slowly and tears began to form. Owen wondered how a wild barn owl could become so dear to this woman. It was another question he would have liked to ask her, but now she was sobbing.

"You okay?" he whispered.

Molly took an awkward step toward him. Owen knew she needed a hug. He had done it before with clients who had lost dogs and cats. It was usually the natural thing to do in his small town practice, where formality was nonexistent, emotional boundaries were for city folk. But, something about this woman suggested to him that a hug would be an act of intimacy. She was not only beautiful, but somehow wounded beyond the owl's demise. He looked over Molly's shoulder and saw Jenny watching him. She, too, seemed to have a sense of something crackling in the air. Owen took his own step forward, closed his eyes, and put a hand on Molly's shoulder. He felt her move into him and then they were hugging as she wept. Jenny looked away in disgust. Owen looked down at the mahogany hair that was suddenly under his chin. It smelled of citrus shampoo and cedar wood smoke. An invisible bridge between strangers was being constructed. Perhaps Roland's barn owl, now streaking into the amethyst light of The Ledge, had left something behind.

The moment came and went with sniffles and apologies from Molly and reassurances from Owen that the owl had most likely died of old age and he would take care of the details. Molly wanted to ask how the bird's body would be disposed of, but decided that it would be too much detailed information to give to the girls. Jenny came in to remind Owen that he needed to close up soon if he was going to meet his friends. The whole incident was wrapped up quickly.

An hour later, Molly Costello was seated at the kitchen counter in Pat Stirling's Fond du Lac bungalow and Owen Palmer was pulling up to the parking lot of a recreational trail near the township of Eldorado. Both of them were still thinking about meeting each other.

"I didn't even know you had a pet owl, Mol." Pat Stirling, who was now Pat Stouffer, shot a thin plume of smoke over her shoulder as she spoke to Molly. Pat and Molly had met when Molly's photographer, Mike Gabler, had swept Pat's daughter, Carrie, off her feet when Molly and Mike had come to Wisconsin to interview Roland Heinz shortly before his death. Mike and Carrie had gone to live in Massachusetts and Pat was forever missing her 'stolen' little girl. Of course, she adored Mike Gabler, but she had hoped for a wedding by now. It had been five years of shacking up with no wedding to plan. Pat never gave up hope for her daughter's marriage, even if she had to settle for getting her friend Molly hitched as a proxy for her daughter.

"It wasn't exactly a pet. It was more like the last vestige of Roland's mark on the farm. The owl merely lived in the barn, but the girls liked it. It's hard to explain, Pat."

"So tell me about this veterinarian. He's a live one, eh?"

Molly knew Pat would ask. She also wondered why Pat had recommended a vet so far out of town. "Have you ever met Dr. Palmer?"

"Actually, I did meet him once when I got my cat at the Humane Society. I think Bim knows him, too. He does some volunteer work there and I got his card. He's rather handsome, isn't he?"

"Hmmm, well yeah. What else do you know about him?"

Pat took a sip of coffee, her prelude to gossip. The cigarette and the caffeine were essential components of Pat's approach to almost everything. Of course, an occasional Old Fashioned worked, too, but that would be later on in the day. She sipped, she puffed, and began. "He's 47, never been married, and lives alone in the apartment above his clinic. Bim's info. He thinks maybe he's gay, but then what the fuck does my husband know about anyone's sexuality?"

Bim Stouffer had been Pat's neighbor two doors down before his wife died two years ago. He had courted Pat almost at the funeral, pleading loneliness and the promise of insurance money to spend. Apparently, Bim had been lonely for most of his marriage, too. Either that or some men just need a wife more than air. Some men were like that. On a spontaneous junket to Las Vegas and after some not so spontaneous drinking, they were married and returned to the gasps and scandalous whispers of the neighbors. Neither of them was fazed and took up their marriages where they had left off. Bim and Pat were like a couple that had been married for many, many years and, in fact they had, though not to each other.

"He's not gay," said Molly matter-of-factly.

"Oh?"

"I can tell if a guy is or isn't. He isn't."

"Well, that's good, huh? So, Molly baby, are you interested? Cuz, if you're not, I got that guy, Junior, from the bowling league hot to take you out. Bim knows him, too and can't stand him. Thinks he's a preening rooster."

Molly smirked and after rolling her eyes around the tidy kitchen she again focused on her friend. "Who has the name

'Junior' in their adulthood, Pat? That's a warning sign right there. I am not going out with anyone named Junior."

"So how about one named Owen?'

Again Molly surveyed her surroundings to gather her thoughts. Pat's kitchen was always spotless even when the rest of the house was a mess. Molly usually never got into the rest of the house for that reason. The kitchen was Pat's office. It was where the coffee pot was. It was where interrogations took place. Bim mostly lived in the garage, where he spent hours sitting in a lawn chair watching the world go by. He practiced his trademark activity year round, which Molly found strange. But, that was Bim. She again focused on Pat.

"Owen's a maybe."

Those words hung in the kitchen air for a moment like the cigarette smoke, swirling lazily towards the ceiling. Pat's eyes seemed to brighten just as Molly's face began to blush. Pat got up and poured more coffee. This conversation was about to get very interesting.

CHAPTER THREE

The first symptom of my mental enigma was sleeplessness. The house, which was bright, cheery, and most of all familiar by day, became strange to me at night. I started to prowl the rooms like a lost child. I took to picking up odd books and reading them by bad light. By odd books I mean texts the kids would bring home from school or ragged paper backs dumped on me by Pat. I had never read romance novels before as I found their formula boring and insulting to women. Now I devoured them like they were forbidden candy. I felt I was regressing; becoming a child again. I thought it was a phase, which all things like this ultimately are, but I began to fear the length of the phase. I began to treat my insomnia like a hidden vice. I made sure I was in bed when the girls got up. I tried to fool them. But then dark circles under the eyes make for a fool's masquerade. I was getting creepy. Even to myself. Something was wrong with me.

The big, tawny cat was getting sick. It was not getting what it needed in the way of food, which made it more desperate and less careful. It had travel far during the winter, vaguely following the direction of the sunrise, employing a pace that mimicked its heartbeat. There had been three of them once, litter mates from a forgotten mother somewhere near a place known to humans as The Black Hills. Perhaps they had originally been distracted by a deer migration that had kept them fed and healthy. Later the three cougars had become lost in the world of modern man. While the farms of Minnesota and Iowa might have provided some food for the taking, they did not provide the cover, terrain, and stalking hunt with which the cats were imprinted. One by one, they had found bridges to cross and had entered Wisconsin by late February. With each strange encounter with man and the machines of his world, the cats' brains began to misfire. Animals that never knew fear began to sense it.

The last river crossing had separated the three cats for good. One had wandered into the Janesville area and was shot by a vigilant farmer. The other walked all the way into the city of Chicago before someone saw it and led it to its fatal encounter with a police swat team in a back alley. Cougar number three, this one, had turned north into the heartland of Wisconsin where white tail deer were abundant and easy to hunt. Without human hunters with which to compete in this season, the cat took what it wanted, when it wanted it. Then it had snowed.

The late winter storm had shut down not only the hunting patterns of the cat, but had left a deep obstacle to her simple movement. The first storm was followed by a second; and then a third. By the time the cat had found the farm of John Oates in Eldorado, it was past hunger and now also losing weight from sickness. On a bright, cold Sunday morning the cat tore open the feeding cage of a Holstein calf, killed and ate it in front of the rest of the herd of dairy cows. While the bleating could be heard for miles, the Oates family was at church during the attack. The neighbors heard nothing as the noise was lost in the stiff morning wind.

John Oates had called the sheriff and eventually the State Animal Control people had been brought in to assess the kill. The large cat prints in the mud and the characteristic kill-from-behind attack left no doubt in anyone's mind that they had a rogue cougar on their hands. The next day a team was assembled to track down the cat and end its reign of terror. It would take two days to gather a sheriff's deputy, an animal expert from the University, and two local vets. One of those veterinarians was Owen Palmer and he was late arriving at the cougar hunt.

Owen found the parked mobile vet truck of his friend, Lee Krieger, along with a car bearing red state tags, and another pickup with a trailer that he didn't recognize. They were just off the county road at the intersection of an abandoned railroad right of way now used for recreation. The sky to the west looked as if rain was coming soon to an already muddy path. He pulled out his cell phone and called Lee, getting a general heading as to where he could rendezvous with the group. They were two or three miles west down the trail. He bundled up against the damp chill and began to walk between the thickets that edged the trail. He noticed there was not so much as a bud on the bushes and trees yet. Not even a bird. Everything was still winter-dead.

He was able to follow the footprints of the others in the mud along with an ATV track. Along the south side of the thicket there was still some dirty snow that the sun hadn't gotten to yet, but then the sun had been absent for days. Owen walked along with his thoughts for what he calculated was about two miles or about a half hour. He could see a long way up the straight line path and still could not spot the others. He was about to call Lee once more when something got his attention. It was a low sawing sound coming from the thicket on his right. In this silent world without so much as a bird song to tickle the ear, he knew almost instantly what he was hearing. He glanced around to locate the exact direction of the sound, but kept moving at a steady pace, although his brain was telling him to run like hell.

Molly had extricated herself from Pat's kitchen and was heading home with her mind whipped by an afternoon of caffeinating and her friend's probing. All the chit chat about men made her uneasy and yet she had surprised even herself by acknowledging Dr. Palmer as someone with romantic potential. Since becoming a fiction writer she had developed the skill of building an elaborate story in her head based on only a vague idea. Methodically, she entertained herself by constructing a simple seduction. She mentally drew up his response. She limned out the romance, filling in details as they streamed into her scenario from her creativity. If her life was a book it would be hers to direct. The character of Dr. Palmer would be heroic; his heart would be pliant to her.

Then another familiar wave washed over her as she rounded the bottom of Lake Winnebago and made the turn north on Highway 151 toward Ghost Farm. It was the feeling that her life was going on mostly inside her head. The characters of her fictions were much more real than they should be. They talked to her. All of them, sometimes all at once. She knew them all as intimately as she did her own girls. And then there was another recurring and disturbing thought: she had given birth to the people who lived in her books while she had merely adopted Sonia and Melanie. Molly flinched as that concept whispered to her. She suddenly realized that she was talking out loud to herself in the car. She had been since she left Pat's house. She also knew it was more than the coffee. It was her obsession to write about things she could not do in her real life. She was falling into the abyss of her own mind, and it was bottomless.

Owen Palmer had walked about fifty more yards when he looked back over his should and saw the cat. His first impression was how large it was and then how yellow its eyes were. Yellow and locked on him. He kept walking and eased the cell phone out of his pocket and rather unsteadily redialed Lee Krieger.

"Lee, I found the cat," he whispered.

"Where are you, man?" Owen could hear Lee shouting at the others in the background. He kept walking at a steady pace. So was the cougar, about twenty paces behind him now.

"I am about two miles from the cars. Jesus, Lee, what should I do? It's stalking me."

"Don't panic."

It was good advice given from a distance. Owen kept walking slowly as reality began to fade away into a nightmare. The scenery started to take on the look and feel of a distant planet. And there was the alien behind him, hunting.

Miles away, Molly went into a full blown panic attack and knew what triggered it. She had let her mind wander too far into the abstract world of her imagination, which, she realized, was no place for a driver to be. At that instant she had been thinking so hard about the next chapter of her novel that she had entered into the book and dropped out of the reality of

staying in her lane on Highway 151. The lapse was only perhaps a nano-second, but it was enough. The daydream was
deep and she couldn't break out of it. She had to slam her
hand into the steering wheel to regain focus. She screamed
as she banged the wheel again. Her heart was pounding and
the adrenaline rush was almost immediate. She hit the brakes
and pulled off onto the shoulder of the road awkwardly, nearly
taking out a mailbox as she slid through the loose gravel. She
was mashing the brake into the floor, bobbing her head up
and down as she counted backwards from one hundred.
Before she got to ninety-five, she was hit by another wave.
This one had the feel of a free-falling elevator, but she managed to put her Subaru Forester into park to take the pressure
off the brake pedal.

The next wave was claustrophobia, so she fumbled out of
her seatbelt and flew out of the vehicle. There, standing on
the side of the road, under the relentless gray skies and in the
persistent easterly wind, Molly Costello burst into tears as
though her heart was pumping salt water instead of blood. A
red-tailed hawk soared above her and shrieked. She instantly
looked up and located the big bird.

"Yeah, I know. I need help."

"Whatever you do, Owen, don't run," Lee Krieger admon-
ished, but it was everything Owen could do to not sprint away
from those yellow eyes that were already tasting him. The cat
was closing now and suddenly the cell phone seemed irrele-
vant. He knew he might need both his hands in the next
instant. As he pocketed the phone, he then remembered he
had a Swiss Army knife in his jacket, and he fumbled for it. As
he opened the two inch blade, he found it almost ironic that
the only tool he had ever used on the knife was the plastic
toothpick. Then he faced the reality that his only protective
weapon was a tiny blade that was more of a letter opener
than anything lethal. He ran through what he knew about
cougars in his head and turned to face his stalker. He knew
the cat wanted him to run so it could take him from behind and
bite his neck. Owen took a little brave breath knowing he was

fit. If it came for him, it was going to be a good fight. He hoped. He suddenly felt no inkling of courage, but he did sense a survival mantle covering his fear. Since flight was not an option, the fight instinct was whispering some long-forgotten battle cry into his ear.

The cougar stopped when Owen stopped and faced him. Owen spoke to the cat. "Hey, you sick old shit. If you're coming, let's go." The cat lowered its head and took a deliberate step towards Owen. Then another. Owen quickly scanned the thickets. Was there a place to retreat? He looked right. Nothing. He looked to his left. Not a break in the brush. He looked behind him for a quick moment and saw figures moving down the trail toward him. He heard the roar of an ATV. The cavalry was coming! He looked back toward the cougar just in time to catch its fury in his arms. Then he was on his back with 115 pounds of feline madness trying to pull his jeans off with her hind paws. The front paws were under his armpits and it was there that Owen felt the first pain as his ribs were scraped. When he opened his eyes, he was looking into the cougar's mouth, which smelled like a sewer.

When Owen smacked the cat's head with his right arm, the hind legs began to churn. He felt pain in his hips and knew it was bad. Then the furtive clawing stopped and the cat began to purr like an old lawnmower. Owen could feel the vibration reverberate throughout his entire skeleton. The cat was now nuzzling him under his chin. He felt the raspy tongue taste his cheek and ear. Owen sensed reluctance in the cat's attack as though it was too sick to fight. And then came the bite.

He was told later by the men who came to save him that all of the attack had only lasted for a few seconds, but it had seemed slow and sequential to Owen. Lee Krieger told him that he was repeatedly driving his tiny knife blade into the cat's neck, but Owen didn't remember any of that. What he did remember for the rest of his life was the feeling that the cat's attack was almost sexual in nature; the weight of the animal on him, the clasping, the awful kiss of death.

When Lee and the others arrived, they were horrified. The Animal Control guy whacked the cat with a heavy ball peen hammer, which stunned it. Lee quickly jammed a syringe of heavy sedative into the cat's neck, while the farmer put a rifle to the animal's temple. Lee pushed it away, protecting Owen first as the cat was already inert. The first order of business was to carefully pry the cat's jaws from Owen's face. One large tooth was lodged in his cheek below his eye and the other long tooth had broken through his front teeth. His lower jaw was unhinged by the bite. Owen was losing blood rapidly from the wounds to his hips and waist and the deep gouges under his arms. His face was a mess. His nose was smashed, and Lee had to get him on his side quickly so the blood and broken teeth didn't choke him.

Owen did get one lucky break in that the medi-vac helicopter that was summoned by the 911 call was already in the area, having just flown another man from a tractor accident to St. Agnes Hospital in Fond du Lac. Paramedics arrived on the scene with the county sheriff and emergency treatment was performed quickly. Owen remembered nothing of his flight for life to Froedtert Medical Center in Milwaukee, but he did remember his dream. He vividly saw the face of the pretty owl woman from that morning standing just behind the cougar's head. She was crying in anguish under the gray skies. He knew she was sobbing because she had seen his face. Or what was left of it.

CHAPTER FOUR

In the darkest night, the one that promises nothing short of annihilation, you dream of perfection in the quick future after death. What a concept. If it wasn't perfect here, then why would it be 'there?' And then a long sigh. The key to everything, everywhere is knowledge. We acquire it slowly at first and then it streams in as though it is in a race with death. We choke on it as our throats contract in old age. Buddhist monks prepare their entire lives for the next one. It seems I have prepared my entire life to wonder about what is going on in this one. I stand in front of a candle, and instead of enjoying the flame, I wonder when it will go out...and what I will do in the dark. I am more of a child than either of my brave daughters.

Karin Salazar was waiting for her sister-in-law, Leah Harrison, at the coffee bar within Borders Books in Goleta, California. She had a latte going, but decided after one sip that she really didn't want it after all. She was starting to feel queasy about asking Leah to meet her there, but it was not so much about the location as the content of their upcoming conversation. Karin was about to make a revelation. She had been keeping a secret, and though it was not particularly a dark secret, it would be enlightening to expose it. Leah was single by divorce and ran a successful art gallery in Santa Barbara. She had become Karin's best friend since Karin's marriage to her brother, James many years ago. Karin had been widow for several years now, and her life had taken a different tack. Instead of plowing on into the future, she was taking a spin into her past. It was a past that only her husband knew of. Both of them.

"Sorry I'm late, Karin," Leah apologized as she began heaping her purse and some boutique bags onto the table. "I lost track of time shopping, as usual. Umm, hi." Leah kissed Karin on the cheek as she made eye contact with the coffee order taker. She and her tastes were known here and the barista quickly went to work on Leah's usual.

"There is no late or early, hon," said Karin, pleased as always to see her in-law buddy. "Anything good in those sacks?"

"Hah, just some junk I couldn't resist. Things that caught my eye ages ago and now..."

Leah paused because she had entered a tricky vein of thought. She was still spending her part of her late brother's estate. James Salazar had been generous to his only sister and even though the sum did not compare to the larger amount Karin had received, she still felt guilty about getting anything. In her mind, the widow should have gotten it all. That would have been fair if that's the way it had happened. However, Jim was a generous and loving man; and a big brother before he was ever a husband.

"Leah, forget it. Jim wanted you to enjoy what he left you. Me, too. So show me."

Leah smiled at Karin. What a gem, she thought for the millionth time. What cloud had her brother found this angel on?

Minutes later, when the coffee was cold and the purchases had been handled and adored, Karin looked for her opening. She began to rock unconsciously and Leah picked it up.

"Okay, so what's on your mind? You want to ask me something, right?"

"Actually..." The word was drawn out looking for its thread. Karin's voice decided to skip past her brain. "Actually, I wanted to tell you something. Maybe ask. Oh, heck, this is crazy."

"What's crazy? Talk to me."

Karin looked into Leah's expectant eyes and thought, okay, she doesn't suspect this. "I was married before."

All she got from Leah was a raised eyebrow.

"I was married back in Wisconsin before I came out here."

Leah was a silent audience. There had to be an upshot.

"I was married to him." With that statement, Karin slid a folded copy of USA Today off of a book that she had hidden beneath it. Leah looked down at the book without moving a muscle. She read the title and author's name. Leah's eyes moved quickly from the book to her sister-in-law. There was a long awkward moment of continued silence. Finally, she took the offered bait and picked up the book. She opened the back cover and looked at the picture of the double Pulitzer Prize winner for literature. It was a later edition of *The Tap Root,* so she was, in fact, looking at one of Mike Gabler's amazing portraits of Roland Heinz.

"You were married to Roland Heinz? Before Jim?" Leah gasped.

"Yes, for a long time, but some of it was not before I met Jim. That is part of what I want to talk to you about."

"You have my undivided attention, Karin." That was an understatement. Roland Heinz was book lover Leah's favorite author. It was a love that she shared with few people. Her immediate emotions were mixed.

"Okay, but let's get out of here. I want to walk while I talk." The bookstore had suddenly become too crowded for secrets.

Meg Bollander looked up from her work, distracted by the sound of a motor outside. Simultaneously, six clocks went off at slightly different intervals to signal it was 11AM. She knew then it was the mailman as she knew everything in her life from the chiming of clocks. Although every hour of her life was chimed in, she no longer cared much about the passage of time. Meg had found an obsession that had replaced her loathing for her one time neighbor, Roland Heinz. With his death five years ago and the subsequent dismantling of the wind turbine on his property that had spoiled her view, she had taken up a hobby. It was something that served to channel her drab existence and squeeze something colorful out of it. The hobby was painting and it was now her passion.

Without a single visitor in five years, no one could have known that her house on The Ledge was now filled with canvasses that Meg had bought from a catalog, had delivered to her house, and had filled with the images that only a mad woman could have captured of the view outside her front window. Her once tidy and knick-knack stocked living room was now her studio. Once polished end tables were now used as palettes to mix her paints. Dirty rags filled the corners. The smells of paint and thinner dominated and cloaked the odors of poor housekeeping and neglected hygiene. The kitchen counters were covered with empty bottles of brandy and whiskey. Meg Bollander's descent into madness had caught itself on a latent talent. She was borderline mad and quite an excellent artist, although not one person had ever seen her work. Then there was a knock on the door. Meg peeked out and saw the mailman staring back at her. Her eyes fell upon a letter that he held in his hand. With a sigh and great reluctance, she opened up a crack in her world.

"Morning, Mrs. Bollander," smiled the carrier.

"What do you want?" Meg frowned. Meg had accepted that most people referred to her as Missus, even though she had taken her maiden name back after a failed marriage.

"Got a letter for you that you need to sign for." The mailman produced an official looking business size envelope. She took it and quickly checked out the return address corner.

"Don't want this."

"Well, actually, you took it into your possession just now so you already have it. Signing is a formality. Maybe it's good news, Mrs. Bollander."

"It's from a lawyer. How's that going to turn out to be good news?"

The mailman suddenly seemed anxious to get away. "It's your business, I guess and I got mine. Here's the rest of your mail." He handed her two other pieces of mail, nodded, and turned away leaving Meg's hand protruding through the crack in her door.

"Hey!' she called as the man was walking away rather briskly. He turned back to face her.

"Yes?"

"What's your name?"

"My name is Norman."

"Norman what?"

"Norman Decourtes."

"You an Indian? I mean they all got Frenchy names, right?"

"Actually, I'm French."

"You new?"

Norman Decourtes took his hat off and ran his hand through his hair. He was a young guy, but he wasn't new. "You asked me that two years ago, Mrs. Bollander. I guess that means I am not new. You know something, I..."

Before Norman Decourtes, the not new mailman, could continue the conversation, the door had slammed shut. He took no offense since the outcome was okay with him. The old folks up here in The Holyland could be eccentric. Meg Bollander was the queen of eccentricity, and he went away thinking he didn't give her long as a customer. She looked like the end of her rope was quite near. Norman, like most mailmen, knew how to read people and dogs.

In the house Meg tossed the registered letter and the other two onto a pile of other unopened mail. She had not even bothered to look at who else was trying to correspond with her besides the Law Firm of Zaneb, Charon, and Marek. Escaping her notice was an envelope shape that would indicate some sort of card. There was no return address label, but the postmark that Meg had ignored, was from Goleta, California.

CHAPTER FIVE

A wise man told me this story: While visiting relatives down South, a young boy was walking near a creek at the back of a large lawn surrounded by woods. A black man was working late trying to get the lawn mowed before the sun went down. Apparently, the mower had disturbed a large red snake, making it aggressive—rising up on its tail like a cobra. The boy watched as the snake followed the man with the mower, obviously meaning to inflict a bite. The mower saw the snake out of the corner of his eye and ducked the first strike. The boy could only watch, frozen in his tracks. When the red snake rose up for its second attack, the black man faced it eye to eye and as the snake leapt at him, he caught the serpent in his fist near the head. The snake writhed with anger, but the man held it until it calmed down. When the snake's ire and menace were gone out of it, the mower set it on the ground and watched as it slithered into the woods. He turned to the watching boy and said. "Boy, every instinct in my soul told me to whip that snake on the ground until it was dead. A million years of instinct said that, son. But, even though that red racer meant me harm, I meant none toward him. The Lord made me think before I acted…and I acted like the Lord." The wise man who told me that story was Owen Palmer.

Owen Palmer remembered very little of his chopper flight from the muddy trail near Eldorado to Froedtert Medical Center in Milwaukee. He vaguely recalled some guy who kept badgering him to talk to him. He knew the guy was trying to keep him from going into shock, but shock and its peaceful blackness seemed like a better place to be at the time than an air ambulance. When he became aware again of being moved, he woke up in pain. His moan seemed to be coming from someone else, but Owen knew it came from him.

"We're at the hospital, Dr. Palmer," said one of the men who were handling him. "These guys'll take good care of you now."

Owen's mind was strobing. He was flashing on the cat and other subliminal events. Somehow he found his voice without thought or effort, although it was weak.

"Don't kill it," he whispered.

"What's that, mister?" Hey, he's talking, Fred."

"Don't kill it," Owen repeated.

Suddenly, from out of nowhere, Owen recognized the voice of Lee Krieger somewhere close by.

"Hey, Owen, you're awake, huh? We're gonna get you fixed up real fast."

"Lee?"

"Yeah, man, it's me. Don't try to talk now, okay?"

Owen felt motion and then the changing of light from dark to bright to dark to bright as he was rushed into the emergency entrance. It seemed surreal. It was. Despite the movement Lee was still there.

"Lee, don't kill it."

Owen opened his eyes and found Lee's face, big as a full moon in front of him.

"Don't kill the cat, Lee."

"I'm not sure what happened to the cat, Owen. It's not important now," said Lee.

Owen felt the prick of an injection into his upper arm. He fought to make this point that seemed more important than his own life at the moment.

"Don't kill the cat. Don't kill it…Lee…don't…" His voice trailed off into the place where his senses had gone to regroup. He thought it might be death, but the owl woman was there. It was good to have company in limbo.

Molly had forgotten to grocery shop that afternoon so dinner was going to be what ever was left over and on the use-or-lose list in the fridge. She found some ham and cheese and just six eggs, but that would make a big enough omelet for the three of them. Melanie was at the kitchen table and had a text book next to her laptop doing something compatible to each. Sony was in the living room watching the evening news as she always did. Melanie's world was all about school, while Sony was a citizen of the world. That world was suddenly loud.

"What?" The shout from the living room startled Molly, though Mel barely flinched. Molly stopped whisking eggs and went to see what was up. As she walked into the living room, her eyes quickly found Sony's pointing finger and followed it to the TV. A lady reporter was standing in front of the emergency entrance of a hospital.

"What's up, honey?"

"Mom, a mountain lion attacked some guy near here."

Molly sat down next to Sony and was trying to get the gist of the news when her cell phone rang in the kitchen. She got up quickly and answered it as she walked back into the living room. It was Pat.

"Molly, put the news on." Pat sounded excited. Molly was confused.

"I am watching the news. What about it?"

"You watching the thing about the cat attack?"

"Yeah."

A loud crash came from the kitchen and Molly rushed back there with the phone in her hand. Melanie's laptop was on the floor with the CD-ROM drive tray broken off. The power cord was looped around Mel's ankle making the cause of the accident obvious.

"Oh, Mom!" Melanie screamed just before a couple of tears burst from her eyes. She moved to Molly for a hug, dragging the injured computer.

"Mom!" Sonia yelled from the living room.

Molly heard a faint noise from the phone and returned it to her ear.

"Molly, you still there?" asked Pat.

Molly felt the sick feeling of panic again beginning to creep over her. Everyone was screaming her name, begging for her attention. She agilely moved from hugging Melanie to escorting her into the living room where they all stood in front of the TV. Nothing was registering, but Pat's slightly digital voice brought her back into focus. She put the tiny phone back to her ear.

"Sorry, Pat."

"Molly? You okay?"

"Yeah, Pat, we just had a little accident with a laptop. No biggie, right, Mel?"

Melanie was now looking at the TV, having switched gears already back to her normal cool.

Pat spoke again. "Then you know, right? You heard?"

"Sorry, Pat, know what?"

"Dr. Palmer."

"Yeah, I know him. Met him today. Remember, I told you all about it."

"Oh shit," said Pat. "Then you don't know."

"Know what for God's sake?"

"The thing on TV about the cougar over in Eldorado. It was him, Mol."

Molly was about to ask another question, but then the light bulb came on in her head. She turned to the TV and stared at the woman reporter who was still standing in front of a hospital emergency entrance. She heard the name 'Owen Palmer' come from the video and nothing else mattered. She snapped the cell phone shut and stepped away from Melanie. The floor began to come up at her, but she willed herself to ride it down.

"What's wrong, Mom?" Melanie asked. Sonia's head swiveled onto her mother also.

"I know that guy." It was the best Molly could do.

"You know the guy who got mauled?" asked Sony.

"How do you know him, Mom?" asked Melanie.

Molly closed her eyes and raised her head toward the ceiling. She suddenly looked almost serene as she tried to clear her head and get a grip on the entire day. The diverging pathways of fate were losing their March overcast and coming into the light. It was at once a horrible coincidence and a bizarre plot twist. As an author she appreciated the complexity. As a woman, lonely and tight-roping over her own madness, she was unexpectedly calm. She opened her eyes. They fluttered.

"I forgot to tell you girls earlier. The owl in the barn died today."

"It did?" said Sonia.

"It was sick and I took it to the vet in Long Lake."

The girls were smart. They knew that even barn owls died. They counted that shoe as they waited for their mom to drop the other one.

"That veterinarian is the same man who got attacked by the cougar or whatever it was. Dr. Owen Palmer. He's a very nice man."

Molly then slowly sat down on the sofa and began to cry. The girls filled in next to her as they all watched the news in semi-silence.

It was a short drive from the bookstore to the park off of Santa Felicia Drive. The soccer fields and baseball diamonds were deserted this time of day giving way to the occasional walker and the sea gulls in their paths. There was an offshore breeze coming down out of the hills to the north and the day was already warm. Karin and Leah always kept their walking shoes in their cars for spontaneous walks.

After a few minutes of silent striding and watching the screaming gulls fight over food wrappers, Leah took Karin's arm and made her stop and face her.

"Okay, I know you are thinking," said Leah. "I can hear the gears grinding in your head. Just let it go, Karin."

Karin smiled weakly. Perhaps she had over-thought this trip into her ancient history. Better to just get it all out. "I want to go back there and I want, I need you to go with me."

"Back there?"

"Wisconsin."

"Oh yes, Wisconsin, where you were married to Roland Heinz before you married my brother."

"You're a quick study, girl." The women resumed their walking.

"Yeah, and you are slow getting to the point," Leah added. "If you're ready, I am."

The story came out finally and lasted two laps of the park.

"I was married to Roland when he got back from Viet Nam and we were okay for a while. The war had taken its toll on him and I tried to understand that. Then came the distance and drinking. We drifted apart. I didn't get pregnant either, which left those bonds untied. I took a job at Mercury Marine in Fond du Lac to get out of the house and away from my husband's moods. It gave me a second life away from home. That's where I met Jim. He was this handsome engineer from the mysterious land of California and our eye contact alone was more romantic than the nights in my husband's bed. I will spare you the details, but I allowed an affair to begin. It was a line I crossed with some guilt, but even greater excitement. Jim was my angel and Roland was my demon. I began to plan the transfer of my heart.

"I allowed the distance to grow between myself and my husband. I began to bait him into arguments. I would sense when he was vulnerable to my wicked tongue lashings and bring him to the brink of violence against me. I wanted that, Leah. If he would only hit me I could be gone. I could leave him and be with Jim. I hated this part of my life, but I had a goal. I wanted out of not only my marriage, but the town, the state of Wisconsin, the state of my mind. Roland's drinking made it easy. You're frowning."

Leah stopped walking and faced her sister-in-law. "We are talking about *the* Roland Heinz, right? How could the man who wrote those books be a drunk, who would hit his wife under any circumstances? This doesn't make sense to me, Karin,"

"Of course not. You are his reader, his fan. He only wrote war stories back then and not very good ones at that. The Roland Heinz you know and love evolved long after I was gone. I still don't know how all that happened, but it did. That is one of the things I want to learn when we go back there."

"I know you have an estranged sister. Is she still there?"

"Well, that's another story and information I need to get. My sister, Meg doesn't answer my letters or phone calls. My fault I know, but I want to repair the damages before it's too late."

"Damages? To her?"

They were walking again.

"My sister was in love with Roland before he and I got married. She made it seem like she was okay with the way things turned out, but I knew she was wounded. He chose me over her after she had done everything to win him. She gifted him her virginity back when it was the act of ultimate surrender to a man. He took it and then I took him away."

"And she never got over it. God, Karin."

"Her love took that turn into hate that so often happens. And then when she thought Roland had beaten me up…"

"So he did take your…your bait and hit you?"

"Big New Year's Eve blow up. I got a broken nose and the broken marriage I wanted. I called Jim and he flew back there to get me. I left Roland, my sister, my job, my old life and got on a plane for the first time in my life. It was a complete escape. I landed here and never looked back until…"

"Until the books."

"I had heard about the first Pulitzer before I had even read *The Tap Root*. I thought what a coincidence, some guy with the same name as my ex is a great writer. Of course, I had to know that for sure, so I hunted down the book and looked at the jacket photo. I was shocked, to say the least."

Leah could only shake her head. She was mentally recalling passages from the book that she adored and now was interpreting them through the lens of this strange conversation.

"And you kept this secret all these years?"

"Well, Jim knew about Roland, of course. The image I had painted to him of Roland did not match the author's image at all. He and I both were stunned. But too much time had gone by since I had known him. Something had happened to Roland, but I was happy with my life so I thought it was a nice upshot."

Leah was anticipating at the speed of light. "Until you thought of your sister."

"Meg. Yeah, I wondered what part, if any, she played in all of this. I wondered, but I didn't do anything about it."

"Until Jim died." Leah was good at this sort of courtroom back and forth. Her husband had been a lawyer before he had left her for a paralegal blonde.

"Leah, it nags at me all the time now. There is a story back there that I was once a part of and then I took myself out of it. I have tried to make contact again with Meg, but no response. I read the Costello articles in *Art Harvest* when Roland died, but they left me with more questions than answers."

"And you know then that Roland Heinz adopted Molly Costello just before his death, right? You know all about that?"

"I know what I have read. None of it computes with my memories of Roland. Anyway, Leah, I want to go back there and get my sister back. I left the old Roland and he died along with the newer Roland. Meg is still alive and I need to try to fix us."

"So when do we go?"

Karin was now smiling without guilt. "As soon as possible?"

"We gonna fly or drive?" asked Leah.

"Road trip?"

Leah's eyes got big in the way travelers do as they contemplate the mythical road." Yeah, let's drive to Wisconsin."

The two women could never know that their final destination was, at that moment, being painted over and over again by the woman of their quest. It was a gray day on The Ledge and Meg Bollander was mixing big daubs of black and white paint with just a touch of cobalt blue.

CHAPTER SIX

I have a clock in my head these days; not the baby-making one, but the one that counts off the time to find true love. Lost chances and false loves of the past seem to be the accelerator in this thinking. I have failed so often that I have to believe there is a flaw in my heart. A hidden filter that will not allow the total release required to love another. I even wondered for a while if I wasn't gay, or frigid, or a just plain, unemotional lump of flesh. My friends told me I was straight because they didn't get the 'vibe.' I figured that out, too, because I really liked sex with men...a lot. So what was it? What is it? More to the point, who is it that is going to find me and give me that one more chance? There perhaps is a face and a name to this phantom now, but maybe I lost him an instant after I found him and identified him. I don't trust myself anymore. I am hopelessly obsessed now with the ticking, but I think I would step off into the abyss for this particular face. Geronimo!

The hot topic around Wisconsin for days was the cougar attack. The main beneficiaries, as per usual, were the press and the merchants selling guns. If there was a one in a billion chance that another cat was roaming around out there, the citizens would be armed and ready to meet it. Owen Palmer, DVM, had become something of a local celebrity, though few folks had known of him before the attack. No one longed for those days more than the victim, wounded by a cat and dogged by the media. His room was guarded at Froedtert as he was being treated against the sepsis from his wounds. Owen was surrounded by IV bags and tubes and now fully alert to his various points of pain. Where he didn't hurt, he itched. Itches caused by scratches, he mused. Then he heard the soft knock of a visitor. He turned his head slightly left and saw Lee Krieger approach his bed with a wary smile.

"You awake?" whispered Lee.

Owen started to speak, but nothing came out. His friend realized this and handed him the plastic water cup. The water tasted funny, but it was ice cold and soothing. It loosened his vocal chords just enough.

"I am awake too much," Owen croaked.

"I can imagine. Lots of people taking care of you, huh?"

"At all hours."

Lee Krieger walked over to the window and looked out. It was mid-morning and the view from the East Clinic looked out toward the modest skyline of Milwaukee. It was a pretty late March morning with yellow, veiled sunshine and purple clouds over Lake Michigan. Owen watched Lee and envied his mobility.

"How's the view, Lee?"

Lee turned and looked at his Owen and saw his face lit now by the morning light. He winced.

"It's nice."

"But, me not so good, huh?"

Lee found the chair near the window and sat down. "That cat got you pretty good. She messed up your good looks, but nothing that can't be fixed. You need to get past this infective stage before you worry about anything cosmetic."

"I suppose."

Neither man spoke as a nurse came in and took Owen's vitals. She checked on his comfort level and departed with a professional smile, nodding at Lee as she left.

"What else can you tell me, Lee?"

"I haven't really spoken to a doctor or anything like that…"

"No, I don't mean about me. What happened to the cat? They kill it?"

Lee Krieger nodded his head absentmindedly and then snapped his head toward Owen as if he had just awakened from a dream. "No, actually the cougar is still alive."

"No shit? How?"

"You probably don't remember coming in here the other night, but you asked me point blank to save the cat. You remember that?"

"No, but I sort of remember thinking it."

"I made a couple calls and the state animal guys had it sedated and in a van headed for Madison. They wanted to do some tests; find out where it came from...how it got here. You know. They were going to draw blood, then kill it and open it up. See what it had been eating. I got a hold of Joe Eptstein and told him your request. You know Joe? He's the head honcho at State Animal. Anyway, he put the whole thing on hold and now your cat is getting treated instead of being euthanized. Nobody knows about this, because the press would be all over it. And there is no rabies, thank God. Lots of other stuff, but no rabies. By the way, you are something of a celebrity now."

"I am? Why?"

Lee scooted the chair a little closer to the bed. "Local veterinarian mauled by rogue cougar. There were three minicam crews out there when I came in. It's a big story, lots of fear and gruesome details. Man versus beast and all that. Cards and letters pouring in here for you."

"Geez, Lee, I don't want that."

Molly Costello sat her kitchen table trying to find the words she wanted to put on a card to Owen Palmer. She was frustrated that the 'great writer' could not even put her thoughts down on a simple, stupid, and generic get-well-soon card. Her youngest daughter, Sonia was watching her struggle.

"Just say what you feel, Mom. That's what you always tell us."

Molly wanted to explain that she had no idea what she was feeling, which was God's truth, but could only nod at Sony's wisdom. She put the pen down and picked up a coffee mug.

"I'll do this later. What are you up to today, honey?" The change of subject perked Molly up. It was Saturday and Melanie was at a meeting at school concerning her advanced program at UW-Madison, leaving her and Sonia to hang out. Maybe.

"I have a date, Mom..."

Molly's head snapped and locked on to Sonia. "A date? With whom?"

Sonia was smiling broadly. She had gotten the effect she wanted from her mom.

"Well…there's this boy I know from school and I am going to watch him work for a while this morning."

"Why would you want to watch him work? And where does he work that you can watch him? And who is he? What's his name?" Molly was suddenly aware that she had taken an interrogative tone. She tried to soften it. "Do you like this boy, Sony?"

Sonia fidgeted, but she was smiling coyly, also. "His name is Hector."

Molly was trying to form a mental image.

"Hector Marquez is his name and he is in my English class. I sort of tutor him," Sonia explained.

Molly was getting the picture now, but was she was wondering why this was the first she had heard of her daughter tutoring someone.

"You are helping him with his English?"

"He's from Mexico, Mom. He actually speaks English great, but he has trouble with all the grammar and spelling and stuff."

"I see. And today you are going to watch him work?"

Well, I may help him work a little, too."

Molly waited for Sonia to go on.

"Mom, he is here with his father and uncles and they work on farms as day laborers. Today Hector is clearing stones out of a farmer's field near Malone and he asked me if I wanted to come along so we could talk about school while he worked."

"And you like this boy, right?" The question was a mother's reflex more than the need for information.

"Okay, Mom, yeah, he's neat. And he likes me. He liked me first."

Molly put her arm around Sonia. She squeezed her baby girl who had now entered a new game. Molly did have the fleeting thought that she was jealous of Sony. Nobody liked Molly first right now.

"Well, I think that is cool, Sony. I actually have met his father, Antonio Marquez at church. We served on a Catholic immigrant orientation committee. He's a very nice man. When do I get to meet Hector?"

Sony thought it over for a predictably long second. "Well, maybe not today, okay? He's picking me up at the end of the drive in a couple minutes. You know."

"I know. Better go. And Sony…"

"Yeah?"

"Have fun picking up fieldstones."

Sonia smiled a smile as if she were going to a picnic instead of a muddy field. "I will. Later, Mom."

As the back door closed behind Sonia, Molly sighed deeply and then looked at the card on the table in front of her. She wondered why she was making this gesture to this man she had only met once. She assumed he was getting cards from all over since everyone was talking about him and the cougar. She wondered what Pat would say. Even though she decided Pat was full of bad advice and reckless romantic notions, she dialed her up anyway. Pat answered on the first ring. Good old Pat.

Donner Pass will always serve to remind travelers on I-80 that they are not really all that hungry. Karin Salazar and Leah Harrison crossed the top of the Sierra Nevada without any comments about the doomed party that made themselves famous by eating one another. There was still quite a bit of snow in the high country and the scenery was keeping them in awe. As Karin's silver 4-Runner dropped into Nevada, the mere changing of states seemed to be the kickoff moment of the real journey. They stopped for gas outside of Reno and then spent a half hour jamming quarters into the slot machines outside the ladies' room. Leah almost seemed embarrassed when she hit three 7's and the machine started dropping quarters loudly into the metal tray. A red light flashed like a police car atop the machine. A few fellow travelers stopped to gape.

"Nice going, Lucky," said Karin, who had no luck at all.

"I never won anything in my life. This is fun." Leah began to scoop the 250 coins out of the tray and load them into a large plastic cup. The idea of a lucky streak did not cross her mind so she got up and left the machine. The two women walked back to the SUV with Leah holding the cup of quarters.

"What are you going to do with that?" asked Karin.

"I don't know…laundry?"

Car doors slammed and they got back on their way across America.

Sonia Costello saw the old Chevy coming down Highway 151 slow down and then stop on the shoulder. The first thing she noticed was that it was full of men she didn't know. She waited until the back door popped open and Hector appeared before she approached the car.

"Let's go, Sonia," Hector said with a shy smile. "Get in."

Sonia again scanned the car. Counting Hector there were already six men crammed in there.

"You sure there's room?"

Hector was fully aware that all the men in the car were making a quick appraisal of Sonia. Most of all, he wanted her to be brave. Sensing this, and frankly without options, Sonia got into the back seat where a space had been made next to a man who appeared to be asleep and a man sitting mostly on the sleeping man's lap. Her first impression besides the closeness was the smell. There was a mix of body odor and tobacco with a hint of stale beer. Somewhere in her memory, the smell was familiar. Hector got in next to her and slammed the door as if securing it from exploding open from inner pressure. The car slogged back onto the highway.

"*Buenos dias*, Sonia," said the driver smiling directly at her from the rear view mirror.

She said, 'Hi."

"That is my father, Antonio. Next to him is my Uncle Leon and Uncle James. And Rudy there, too. This is Manny and Manny," indicating the men on her right. Everyone except the sleeping Manny said hello and smiled. Someone said something in Spanish to Hector and they all laughed.

"What'd he say?" asked Sonia.

"He said you have been in the sun longer than he has," explained Hector.

"Oh," said Sonia, feeling a little self-conscious now.

"No, Sonia, it's okay. They are not being…racist." He whispered the last word. "He also called you *bonita*, which is beautiful."

Sonia nodded and tried to just look out the window, but her eyes kept stealing glances at Hector. She thought he was *bonita*, too.

It was only a short ride to the field near Malone where the men would spend their day. A tractor and a flat-bed wagon were waiting for them along with a man that Sonia assumed was the farmer. Hector's father shook hands with the man; heads nodded. She noticed that there was money passed even before the work. Sonia took this as a sign of trust and felt good for the workers. As Hector's father started up the tractor, the men fell in line flanking it. It was then that she noticed how many stones were in the field—it was covered with them. She looked at Hector as he handed her a pair of gloves.

"You can either walk along and watch or help," he said, but the gesture of the gloves indicated what he expected from her, she thought.

"I came to work," said Sonia. Soon she was imitating the labor of the men; stooping, lifting, and loading stones onto the wagon. The morning was cool and she found she liked the hard work. She liked being with Hector and these men who did not shirk at the task before them. When her cell phone chirped, she saw their heads turn to her. It was her mom and she knew she had to answer it.

"Hi." The greeting was almost cold. "Yes…no. It's okay. I can't talk. I'll call you later….I don't know. Up by the wind farm near Malone. Yeah, okay, Bye."

Sonia switched the ringer off and put the phone in her jacket pocket. For an instant she felt spoiled and alienated from the group. "Sorry, Hector, it was my mom. You know."

Hector heaved a stone onto the wagon as he spoke. "You are lucky. To speak to my mother I have to find a pay phone that works and then plug in the numbers of a phone card. Then wait and hope she is home."

"Where is she? I mean I know in Mexico."

"Nuevo Laredo."

Sonia nodded and resumed her work. She noticed that their line was taking them right up to one of the huge white wind turbines. She thought they looked so much bigger up close than they did from the road. The blades were turning slowly facing the west, where the breeze came from. The sun behind the tower was casting a shadow and the blade shadows were making her dizzy. She concentrated on the field stones until they were past the huge tower, but the throb of the turbine made her nervous. It was so foreign and powerful, she thought. And they were turning in every direction she looked. The wagon was filling with stones.

CHAPTER SEVEN

The best part about being a writer is the intimacy with the page. Sometimes the keystrokes are like kisses even if the thought doesn't work or the metaphor is hopelessly mixed. I used to be too stylized as I made my pitch to the page. I was lofty at first and then I remembered my adoptive father and relaxed into honesty. I did find out that this honesty did not always sell, but who do I compete with, anyway? My only failure as a fiction writer so far is that I have not found my Garnet Granger, my other self, who will go a' haunting pages with me. I tend to write characters that I have known too much, too well. What I need is to find that certain spirit that I have never, could never, have known before in my own life. Perhaps when I do, I will cross that borderline that Roland skipped across. My greatest fear is that his painful life was the only path to Garnet. I am not sure I am ready for that kind of pain.

Sometime before midnight on Sunday, Owen Palmer became very sick. He felt it coming on in his sleep, a rush of nausea and panic. He was barely aware that he had vomited or nearly thrown himself out of his bed. He heard beeping alarms as his blood pressure either soared or dove. He did feel a gust of cold air and felt as though he was floating.

When he opened his eyes he was sitting in his apartment above his veterinary practice in Long Lake. It was like being placed within a theatrical set on the darkened stage of a play with no audience. His brain told him in very clear 'words' that he was dying. It seemed logical and expected and he surrendered to the concept, but then he realized he was not alone. There, sitting at his kitchen table was the owl woman. She was crying. He wondered a vague how and why and, as if hearing him, she looked across the room at him and spoke:

"I don't want to go out with Junior," she said matter of factly.

Owen was surprised at the clarity of her voice. He wondered if she were dead, too.

"Who's Junior."

"Bim says he's a rooster."

"Who's Bim?"

"The man who sits in the garage all the time," answered the owl woman. "If you die, I have to marry Junior and he will sit in the garage, too."

"I think I may already be dead. I'm sorry."

The owl woman looked at him and shook her head in an exaggerated fashion. "No, you're not dead yet. Why would you say that?"

"Because I am talking to you…here."

The owl woman's face became quizzical as though she did not understand his logic. She sighed. Suddenly the room turned upside down and the floor became the ceiling. The lady at the table was still sitting at the table, but she was now hanging from the ceiling, mahogany hair spilling down. He felt strong hands gripping him, moving him, shaking him. He smelled the cougar's breath. Everything faded to black.

What followed was yet another series of dreams populated by specters dressed as nurses and doctors. Time was measured by sudden awakenings and flashes of bright light as he was treated, cleaned, and medicated. Owen began to understand that he was going to live because he sensed a letting up in the intensity of his care. Another sure sign was the movement of his bowels once again. Once when he was being helped from the bathroom back to his bed, his doctor was waiting for him. Dr. Foreman was a round, balding man with a very red neck. He looked trustworthy, kind, and ready for his own coronary.

"Hello, Owen," said Dr. Foreman. "Good to see you moving around."

Owen was dizzy from moving around, but managed a smile.

"Everything in the room is moving, Doctor."

"Give it time. We pumped enough drugs in you to start a pharmacy."

A nurse situated Owen back in his bed, reattached his IV, and left the room.

"What was it, Pasteurellosis?" Owen asked.

"Your diagnosis is correct, Doctor. I have never dealt with it before. Nasty stuff."

"Well, pet cats can carry it so why not a cougar? What's next?

Dr. Foreman came around to the window side of the bed and pulled up a chair.

"We're moving you again."

"Madison?"

Dr. Foreman nodded.

"University Hospital will be a better fit for you in a couple ways, including your continuing insurance coverage. I'm sure you know that. But, mainly, now that you are getting stronger you need to have several skin grafts and someone will need to fix your face."

Owen nodded, but said nothing. He had seen his face in the bathroom mirror and could imagine what was ahead just to make him half-way presentable. The sores on his hips and torso were still raw and painful.

"Mathisson over at UW is one of the best reconstruction guys in the country. He literally wrote the book, Owen. Ever hear of him?"

"Not in my field, but I trust your word. When am I going over there?"

"Ambulance is coming for you first thing in the morning. They want to work you up ASAP. That sound okay?"

"I guess so."

Dr. Foreman stood up and held his hand out to Owen. The two men shook hands.

"Owen, I got the biggest cliché in the world for you, but you need to hear it anyway. You're a lucky man. If that cat had been rabid we probably aren't talking to each other, okay? If the flight for life wasn't in the area, you don't make it either."

Owen managed a wry smile.

"If I'm not out on that path, I don't meet the cougar. What kind of luck was that?"

"Don't know. Maybe it was fate, but you made it back from a tough spot. Good luck with the rest of it."

The men nodded silently and Foreman left the room leaving Owen to contemplate fate and luck. He instinctively touched his cheek and felt a bubble of scar tissue over a wound. Despite the areas of pain and the mild feeling of nausea, he entered a moment of peace. His survival had just sunken in and it came on a wave of thankfulness and some vague feeling of being loved. He awoke again a few hours later to begin his journey down I-94 to Madison.

Melanie Costello sat in the back of the SUV and looked out the window as Columbus, Wisconsin went by. Actually, it was only green signs that promised a Columbus if you got off Highway 151 and drove a few miles into it. The scenery was that of the endless parade of tidy Wisconsin farms as the road ambled toward the capital of Madison. She was on an orientation trip to the University with three other brainiacs who were too smart to stay in high school. She took a little pride in the fact that they were all girls and at least two of them were friendly. The one that was distant was the other Asian girl. Melanie was Vietnamese and this girl was Chinese. Melanie was pretty and this girl was plain, which Mel thought might be the problem. The two other girls were both very friendly and talkative. Mel liked to talk, but she liked to listen even more. Listening had served her well because she absorbed everything she heard and remembered it. Her IQ made her an information sponge and data was the key to higher education. At least that was her assessment. If you never forgot anything you learned you could tap into it.

One of the persons in the front seat was Ms. Castalone, a guidance counselor from Fond du Lac High School. The driver was a grad student from the University, Sam Somebody-or-other. Melanie was thinking that he was driving a little too slowly. She was daydreaming about Madison and wanted to get there.

"Hey, Planet Earth to Melanie," said one of the girls, Amber, who was from Melanie's high school.

"Huh?" said Mel, coming out of her reverie. Everyone giggled, even the other Asian girl.

"Sarah asked you if you had a boyfriend," said Amber.

Melanie saw the driver glance at her in the rear view mirror. Ms. Castalone seemed interested in her answer, too.

"No, no boyfriend," said Mel, but blushed anyway. She thought they wanted a further explanation, but she decided to shut up and smile along with the rest of them. Besides Columbus and few thousand dairy cows, there was a future out there on this highway; the same highway that ran past the Ghost Farm. Highway 151, Military Road: the magic concrete carpet.

When the fieldstone laden wagon was filled to the point that it was too heavy for the tractor it had to be unloaded. Stones that had lain scattered long ago by the glaciers now were stacked at the edges of the farmer's field waiting to become a rustic wall. Sonia was tired before the first such wagon was unloaded, but she worked on. A song was singing in her head. It was the song of her own people. Poor people of the Sudan clearing land and turning sweat into food. Hector and his people saw Sonia's will and she became one of them. Stoop, lift, move on to the next. It was a rhythm she understood and nothing after that day would be the same. She decided that she loved Hector partly because he was working so hard for his mother in Mexico. She admired all of them, set in their task and not complaining one bit. But there was another place in her that had been awakened and it was far away in Africa. These simple men picking stones out of a field so they could support families in another country struck a chord. A homeland had always been a fuzzy concept to her, but now it was coming into focus.

At lunch time she shared their tortillas and fruit. Some of the men drank from a paper bag, but Sonia saw that it made them happy and energetic, not drunk. The second half of the day went quickly and soon it was over. She rode back to

Ghost Farm not as a stranger, but as a compadre. The car waited as Hector walked her up the drive to the house. Sonia Costello got her first real kiss from a sweaty boy with skin almost as brown as hers. So many things had happened to her heart in the course of that day that telling them to Mom just didn't seem right. Besides, she was sore and tired to the core. A shower was essential. Sleep was ecstasy.

Melanie lay awake in the dorm room in Chadbourne Hall where she and the other girls were spending the night. Amber was her roommate and had been up reading until just ten minutes ago and now was snoring softly. There were lots of strange noises and muffled voices coming in from the hall and they all were stimulating Melanie's imagination. It was spring break at the University, but the dorm was never empty or closed during the year. The dorm was a fluid, restless place of humming college life and she liked being there. She was almost ready to go to sleep after pondering the scheduled activities for the next day when there was a loud crash outside the door. The noise was followed by a girl's laugh; another girl's 'shush,' and then giggles. Amber's head popped up in the semi-darkness.

"What was that?" asked Amber, now awake.

Melanie got out of bed and crept over to the door. She listened for a moment and then slowly opened it a crack and peeked out. She was looking at two young women sitting on the tiled floor. They smiled when they saw her; smiles followed by laughter.

"Oops...sorry," snorted one of the girls.

"You guys okay?" asked Mel. She could already smell the beer.

"We're locked out," said one of the girls as she awkwardly stood up. "Can we crash in your room?"

Amber was now standing with Melanie. "Can't someone let you into your room?" asked Amber.

"Well, that's the tricky part," said the other girl. "We're lost, too." With that statement both of the girls in the hallway looked at each other and burst out laughing. Before Melanie could react, Amber had motioned them in.

Melanie took on the role of detached observer during the next ten minutes as Amber quizzed the tipsy girls. Nothing was learned or settled except for the fact that the girls still had several cans of beer in their purses. When they offered beers to Mel and Amber, Melanie declined and got back into her bed. Before she closed her eyes, she heard the whoosh of pop-tops and saw Amber kiss the forbidden can.

Melanie thought that morning came unnaturally fast and was awakened by a soft knock on the door. She quickly looked around and saw the two night visitors were gone. Amber was still asleep. She went to the door and opened it to see their chaperone, Ms. Castalone frowning and tapping her watch.

"You ladies are supposed to be downstairs and ready to roll."

Melanie frowned and shook her head to clear it. "We had a lot of noise here last night. Sorry. We'll be down in five minutes."

Ms. Castalone turned away and Melanie went over to nudge Amber. Not a good start, she thought. Neither girl noticed the discarded beer cans in the waste basket.

CHAPTER EIGHT

I went to a movie alone last week. I hadn't done that in ages. We usually rent movies at home; the ones that were released months before and now line the shelves at rental stores. Small screen stuff with marginal entertainment value and little or no sensory impact. Some good films require a big screen and an auditorium to have their effect. At least that is how it was when I was growing up in Boston. I guess I went to the movies to try to find Boston and maybe have a little cry. I guess I was homesick. The old ornate movie houses like those in my old neighborhood are gone, replaced by these cinderblock Cineplex's. Popcorn is outrageously over priced. Actors are wooden. Scripts are stock. Directors lack imagination. Audiences lack self-control. My night out alone in a theater lacked even more than all of that combined. It lacked a shoulder warmly leaning against my own. The bad, sad movie might have transcended all the other charmless trappings if there had only been a shoulder. I cried on the way home.

It was an unusually warm spring day for Wisconsin, and while Bim Stouffer did not require warmth for his garage sitting, he did enjoy it. Bim was into his third beer at 10 AM and was listening to a particularly strong solo from a cardinal somewhere across the street. The branches were still bare, but he couldn't quite locate the bird. His squinty-eyed concentration was broken by Molly's car pulling up in front of the house. Bim couldn't help but notice that Molly avoided him. She never pulled into the driveway and never came around to the back door, although he held out hope that she would someday.

As Molly crossed the driveway heading for the front door, he called to her, "Hey, Molly, you got a minute?"

Molly smiled, but kept going until Bim yelled louder. "Hey Miss Perfect, com'ere once."

Molly stopped and looked at Bim, then looked around for someone to save her. Seeing no such person, she changed her course and wandered carefully down the driveway to the perpetually open garage.

"Why Miss Perfect, Bim? You trying to pick a fight?"

"Naw, Molly, just trying to get your attention is all. Wanna beer?"

Molly glanced quickly into the garage while she composed her refusal. There was a car covered by a canvas tarp on one side and most of the rest of the space was filled with assorted boxes, yard tools, and standard American garage junk. She glanced down at the cooler next to Bim's folding lawn chair and saw two dead soldiers next to it. She assessed the situation immediately.

"Thanks, but no thanks. Too early for me. Gotta talk to your wife, anyway."

"She ain't home."

"She's not? I talked to her earlier and she said come over anytime."

"She went to Fleet Farm to get some udder balm."

"Udder balm?"

Bim leaked a wry smile. "Just funnin' you, Mol. Have a seat here for a minute. She should be back any second."

Molly looked at the other vacant chair as if it were the electric version on death row. She had never ventured into Bim's world before. In fact, she had never seen him in the house. He was always the entity in the garage. She never quite understood the arrangement, especially from Pat's perspective, but then it was none of her business, anyway. She slowly sat down on the other side of the cooler and beheld the view.

"So this is your world?"

"Yeah. Hey, Molly, you hear that bird across the street?"

Molly listened and instantly heard the distinct song. "Cardinal, right?"

"Right, but can you see him? My eyes ain't what they used to be."

Molly quickly located the bird high in a bare elm tree: red on black against blue.

"I see him. Up there" She pointed and Bim followed her finger.

"Oh yeah. Good eyes there Molly."

"You can call me Miss Perfect."

"Not gonna drop that one, eh? Sure you don't want a beer?"

Molly was about to turn him down again when a black squirrel appeared scrambling up the driveway toward them. The squirrel stopped, looked around, and then took a copious pee on the broken pavement. After a moment of mutual stunned silence, they both laughed out loud.

"You see that, Mol? If that ain't a sign to have a beer, I swear I never seen one."

Sometimes one just has to bow before twisted logic. "Just one, Bim. That little shit made me thirsty."

Twenty-five minutes later Pat's car pulled into the drive-way and she got out with a bag of groceries and a smirky smile.

"He seduced you, too, huh? Jesus, Molly, it ain't even noon yet."

"Noon schmoon," said Bim.

"I hope you know you just destroyed your reputation, Molly," said Pat.

Molly's second beer, the birds, and the squirrel had led her to a place of refuge from her usual prison of morning anxiety. It was a spell she knew she had to break, but it was so pleasant to have a beer buzz among friends on a warm spring morning that propriety meant nothing to her right then.

"We are just watching the wildlife, Pat. Join us?"

Pat set her bag down and found another chair. She placed it next to Molly facing the street. Bim handed her an opened beer as she crossed her legs and lit a cigarette.

"If you can't lick 'em, join 'em, eh? What wildlife?"

Bim leaned forward and spoke in a conspiratorial tone. "Birds, squirrels, and maybe a cougar, huh Molly?"

The nerve was struck, but it was the nerve Molly had come over to soothe with her friend. She had planned to talk over coffee, but fate had stepped in as it always did and Bim had gotten the first shot. She felt both of the Stouffer's waiting for her to respond. All she could come up with was a 'yeah' followed by a gulp of cheap lager.

The border between Wyoming and Nebraska was a true border: the end of the West and the beginning of the Prairie. There were still a couple of landmark rock formations in Nebraska, but the mountains were gone along with most of the postcard scenery. Karin and Leah had gotten up before the sun and now an hour into this leg of their trip, it was hitting them square in the face near Scott's Bluff. So was reality.

"Leah."

"Hmmm?"

"We're in Nebraska and I'm starting to chicken out."

Leah looked up from a road map that was in her lap. "I wondered when this moment would come. I kind of figured it would be about the half way point."

Karin glanced over at her and then put her eyes back on the road. "Yeah, weird, huh? I mean, I have no idea all of a sudden why I want to do this. It seemed like a good idea back home. Find my sister, put things right, but now…"

"Now that we are getting closer, it seems unreal, right?"

"Exactly."

"Do you want to turn around?"

"Yes, I mean no. Help me, Leah."

Leah folded the map and put it into the glove box, shutting it rather hard, but in a way that Karin recognized as a prelude to straight talk. Leah had a look that was both questioning and firm.

"As I recall," began Leah, "you…we are going back to solve a mystery. What happened to your ex-husband to make him a great writer and what happened to your sister along the way? Is that correct?

Karin nodded, eyes still on the road.

"Well, you know if you turn around, all that will be nagging you to the grave. You need to know all this or you'll drive yourself nuts. Let's go, find out what you need to know, and drive home. End of story."

"But, you must understand that I am returning to the scene of my own crimes. No one is sitting back there waiting to welcome me home, you know."

Leah was mute for a moment as she went for a working angle.

"Do you believe in fate, Karin?"

Karin glanced over in rhetorical silence.

"Back there in Goleta you put this little arrow into a bow and shot it off. I would guess it is in mid-arc right now. No matter what, it has to come down to earth. I think we should find out who or what it strikes when it does. It is your fate to know. It's my fate to witness."

"I get your point, but it sounds even hokier now."

"I never was good at metaphors. How about this approach? I have never been to Wisconsin. I want to meet my sister-in-law's sister. I want to know everything there is to know about Roland Heinz. I, I, I. Me, me, me."

Karin looked over and smiled. "Okay, Mimi, you convinced me. I'd do anything for you, you, you."

"Good, then find me a rest area. I have to pee, pee, pee."

The North Platte River was crossed in lieu of the Rubicon.

Molly and Pat had excused themselves from Bim's morning party and went back in Pat's kitchen, Molly's confessional booth of choice. Tea seemed a better chaser than coffee for the beer and there was a plate of fresh-baked oatmeal cookies between them. Pat munched one, as she listened to her friend.

"I sent him a card. What else could I do?"

"That's a good start."

"It's a start and a finish, Patty. I don't know him. I only met him once. I don't know any of his friends. I am worried about him, but there is no way to find out how he is doing or anything. Maybe I should go out with Junior what's-his-name."

Pat smiled. "Forget Junior. Forget I mentioned him."

"Why, is he really as bad as Bim says?"

"I don't know," Pat said absent-mindedly. She picked up the newspaper and shook it out and folded it to reveal an article and then shoved it under Molly's nose. "Cougar Victim Moved To Madison."

Molly glanced at the article and let out a low 'Hmmm.'

"Hmmm what, Molly? Now you know where he is."

"'Hmmm' is code for thinking that Dr. Palmer and my daughter are both at the same place."

"Mel is in Madison?"

"She went down for some sort of orientation. She called me this morning and said they were going to get a tour of University Hospital today."

Pat seemed pleased that her piece of intelligence matched Molly's information. "Molly, my dear, do you believe in magic?"

Melanie Costello was given a doctor's coat and a name badge, both of which made her feel special as she and the other girls toured University Hospital. It was a five hour tour with lunch breaking up the day. In the cafeteria she noticed a lively group of people taking up several tables. They had laptops set up and there were some video cameras set up in front of a backdrop that had the UW Hospital logo. Melanie was curious.

"Who are those people?" Mel asked her guide, who was an intern named Robert.

"Oh, those are the TV news crews from Milwaukee and Madison. They've been buzzing around here all day."

"Why?"

"The guy who was attacked by that cougar about ten days ago is now here. He was sent over from Milwaukee this morning. I guess that's news," Robert added.

"That happened near where I live," said Melanie. "My mom knows the man who was...attacked."

She had stumbled, not over the word 'attacked,' but the exaggeration that her mom 'knew' Dr. Palmer. Mel was smart and quickly realized that her talk could get her in front of those cameras if she wasn't careful. Fortunately, the remark had gone over Robert's head and they were soon back on tour of various departments. At least they were until fate stepped in again, darting like an imp and knitting up coincidences into the strange cordage of life.

A half hour before the girls were scheduled to head back to the dorm, and then out to dinner, they passed through a patient ward on the 5th floor. Melanie had excused herself to use a restroom and was catching up with the group when she passed a man in a wheelchair in the solarium at the end of the hall. The weak spring sun was making its way down into the trees of Madison and the pink light was on the face of the man. His eyes were closed, but his chin was raised as if meeting the light and drawing it into him. The face was ravaged and Melanie instantly knew who she was looking at. Against her better judgment, she cleared her throat and said a soft 'hello.'

The man opened his eyes, saw her, and fashioned what looked like a painful smile. "Hello," he said.

"I, I know you are Dr. Palmer," she stammered. She looked around, hoping she wouldn't get in trouble talking to a patient. They were alone.

"Yes, I am. And you are?"

"My name is Melanie Costello. You met my mom on the day..."

"Your mom?" Owen was looking at the pretty Asian girl and trying to remember who he had met 'on the day.' Costello did sound familiar.

"My mother is Molly Costello. She..."

"The owl!" he interjected.

"Yeah."

"And you are her daughter?"

Melanie realized the confusion now. "Her adopted daughter." She smiled in a way that soothed Owen like a pain killer. It was pure sunshine.

"She sent you a card at the other hospital, but maybe you didn't get it."

"Melanie, I haven't really had a chance to read much of anything. Tell her thanks for me, okay?"

"Okay. I should get back to my group. I'm sorry if I disturbed you. I felt like I should say hello for my mom."

Owen spun his chair around so he was facing Melanie directly. "Are you going to talk to your mom today?"

"I call her all the time."

"Good. Tell her I dreamed about her when I was really in a bad place and she…"

Melanie waited for him to finish.

"I don't know how to say this…she helped me. It was like she shared my delirium."

At that moment Melanie saw Amber waving at her from down the hall.

"I gotta go," Mel said.

Owen nodded.

"But, I'll tell her what you said."

They smiled and ended their moment of fate.

CHAPTER NINE

Picture me in the doorway between the kitchen and the living room watching my youngest child engaged in a courting ritual with a young boy. They were watching a reality TV show, using it as an excuse to tease each other and lean their bodies together while laughing. Normal stuff...yes, but it made a thought ignite in my brain that was at first delightful and then disturbing. In that instant, I realized that I had only been renting my adopted daughters. Not only that, but there were biological mothers either alive or dead that would never see their babies grown into womanhood. I knew the world of reality TV never would follow the war-ravaged families of Darfur or Viet Nam. Sponsors wouldn't be able to sell burgers and cereal in the breaks between the giggles and the suffering. Maybe I am getting too serious—or too careful? And these simple things are slowing down my smiles.

There was lull in the day; something so subtle that only the eye of an artist who painted the same landscape over and over again would notice. A cloud so soft and slightly purple had swept in from the north and it was doing things to the setting sun that she had never seen before. Meg Bollander cocked her head as if to grasp its nuance as it influenced a world of which she had become an expert observer. The cloud befuddled her. What colors of paint could she mix to imitate it? She went to the window to peer out at the entirety of the cloud and then realized how dirty the window had become. Stains on the inside were combining with water marks and dirt to distort her sense of color. It had to be fixed. Meg's search for window cleaner took her under her sink: a place not visited in years. Even mice could not have survived amid the toxic mixture of spilled chemicals, lime deposits, and sour must and there was evidence of that. An ossuary of rodent bones lay among tufts of hair, giving the under-sink the look and smell of a freshly opened Egyptian tomb.

Eventually she found a half bottle of Windex and a half bottle of stale brandy. After pouring the sadly useless brandy into the sink, she went back to her picture window and applied the cleaner and a rag to the glass. What happened next as Meg wiped the window ruined her day. She realized quickly that her lens to the world had been distorting it badly. Once clean, the view, the cloud, everything had changed color. This revelation drove the artist to the good brandy.

As her drink began to make its familiar warm flow through her body, something unfamiliar began to happen to her soul. Somewhere deep inside the act of cleaning the window triggered the mechanism that allowed her to clean her eyes. Meg Bollander, the watcher and painter, began to weep. It came first in mere tearing and then convulsed her chest. Her head began to nod as if acknowledging the emotion as a long lost friend. She pulled her afghan up to her neck and shivered beneath it. She closed her eyes and felt the tears slide down her face arriving at the corners of her mouth. She tasted them and knew that they were the opposite of her liquor: purity to poison. In some unexplained way she understood that both liquids could exist in harmony in her world, though one had been missing too long.

When her 'good cry' had ended, she stood and wandered around the old house, turning over the debris, looking for something missing. She went into her bedroom that she never used anymore, having adapted to sleeping for years in her chair. The room was filled with finished canvases, mostly small, but a few were large panels leaning against the walls. Art supplies in various states of depletion covered her dresser and the bed. Dust balls filled the corners and paint-stained rags covered the rest of the floor. Meg tossed some small paintings aside and opened the drawer of what once had been her bedside table. In the drawer was a copy of Roland Heinz's last book, *The Needle's Eye*. She knew that the time to begin it had arrived with the tears and the new light coming through her picture window.

In the course of the last few years, Meg had taken a solitary journey into the world of alcoholism and loneliness. She had walked the same path Roland had walked only in the opposite direction; he emergent and she absorbent. Though no one, including herself, knew or cared where she had arrived, anyone with even a modest knowledge of art would have looked at all the scattered lake-scapes that filled the house and would have recognized that Meg Bollander had become every bit the artist that Roland was. Though no longer of the same world, they both had made great art out of great pain. Meg lived alone in an undiscovered treasure trove.

She again made herself comfortable and, though driven to paint almost every night, she now sipped her drink, pulled up the afghan snuggly, and cracked the spine of Roland's tome. She began to read:

> *Garnet Granger watched the Perseid meteor shower from the bottom of Lake Winnebago; the lake water being amniotic in its warmth and peacefulness. The streaking stars glyphed in her brain and became words of cold fire. The words were stroked on the page of the sky by a bony hand, though the style was swift and sure, causing her to sigh so deeply that the passing fish came by to kiss her cheek in harmonic empathy.*

Meg fell asleep before she finished the first page. Roland's words were such a strong narcotic. And in that night March became April.

Molly had been expecting a check-in call from Melanie to let her know when she would be back in town. The call came with Melanie-like promptness right around noon on Sunday.

"Hi honey, how's Madison?" As she spoke, Mollie managed to hook the cell phone under her chin while she wiped off the kitchen counter. The speaker phone option had never appealed to her.

"It was pretty good. I learned a lot, I guess."

Molly recognized the guarded tone in her daughter's voice. Something was up. "You guess, huh? What's going on, Mel?"

There was a pause in Melanie's delivery. Thoughts were gathered. "Mom, I have good news and bad news. Which do you want first?"

This little word game was one that Molly hated to play, but she went along with it this time. "Okay, I'll take the bad news first. Shoot."

"Well, you are probably going to hear about this from Ms. Castalone anyway. Okay, long story short, okay? Someone found some beer cans in the trash can in our dorm room and it was all a big mistake."

"Whose mistake, Mel?"

"Well, it's kind of a long story, but some girls came to our door during the night and were sort of lost and had been drinking. Mom, they were locked out of their room, so me and Amber let them in. They had some more beer on them and they drank some more in our room."

"Oh, Mel, do you know how that…"

"Mom, I went to sleep. I didn't drink anything. Should we have turned them away?"

Molly was trying to recreate the scenario in her own mind. She trusted Melanie implicitly in all things. This was the first crack in that trust and she did not want to overreact and come off as a member of the prosecution. And yet, wasn't this her biggest fear of Madison coming true on the first trip down there? UW had a party school reputation to which Melanie was naïve. She also sensed something already being hidden in the story. Two quick dots were connected.

"Let me guess…you didn't drink, but Amber did?"

"Mom…"

Melanie had answered the question and defined the issue. She was being asked to lie about her program partner; to put all the blame on the night visitors. Melanie, more than anyone, knew this kind of justice was false. Minor things always grew larger when they were covered up. In this case an elite scholarship was hanging in the balance for both girls.

"What am I going to hear from Ms. Castalone?" Molly asked.

"She wants to meet with you and Amber's mom."

"How much trouble are you in?"

"I don't know, Mom."

"Are you planning on lying for Amber?"

Silence on Mel's end.

"Okay, we'll talk about this later. You gonna call me when you get back to the school?"

"Yes, Mom."

The dejection and conflict in Melanie's voice came into Molly's ear crystal clear. It hurt to hear it.

"Okay, listen, babe, I love you. Cheer up. This is going to be okay. We'll work it out together. Got that?"

"I love you, too, Mom. I'll call you from school."

"Okay." Molly waited for a reply, but the connection was gone. Then she remembered the good news part of the call and redialed Melanie's cell phone. Mel answered immediately.

"You want to know the good news, right?" asked Mel.

"Hey, after that little bombshell…"

"Mom, you're not going to believe this, but I met the man who got mauled by that cougar."

Molly's tailbone hit the bottom of the wooden kitchen chair rather hard as she made an awkward and fast landing on it. "You met Dr. Palmer?"

"Yep, he's at UW Medical Center now."

"How is he, I mean tell me what he said."

"He looks real bad, Mom, but he was very nice. I told him that you were my mom and that you had met him earlier, you know, that day. He said he remembered you and our owl. He said you helped him."

"I helped him? What does that mean?"

"I don't know, but that's what he said. He said to say hello to you and you know, he really meant it. I could tell."

Suddenly Molly had way too much to think about. She needed to get off the phone, maybe go for a walk. "Okay, thanks, Mel. We'll talk some more later. We'll talk a lot later."

"Okay, bye, Mom."

Again the connection went dead as Molly came to life.

CHAPTER TEN

I am above the weather today. I see a bright sun in my mind although there is only a gray pearl above the barn this morning. Some days are full of possibilities and this might be such a day. When I have this feeling, I hold it close; shine it up like a sterling cup. I know that my sadness has only been thinly covered, but I love that cover when it comes off. But then, just writing these lines makes my soul try to eclipse my sun; makes me doubt myself. Trusting myself has been hard lately. Trusting feelings seems phony. And yet, the idea that someone out there across the marshes, moraines, and muddy creeks might be thinking about me is building a castle in my heart. The citadel is lovely in the sunlight, but please God, don't make the walls too strong. When and if the siege comes, I want them to crumble as though they were made of sugar.

Karin and Leah were following the Platte River as it wound from Lincoln, Nebraska up to Omaha. Although there was still very little spring greenery along the river, the sky was telling a different story. Dark, ominous clouds had moved over them and now, in the late afternoon, they took on a drab olive hue that usually meant trouble. Cars coming toward them on I-80 had their headlights on and seemed to be wet. There was a rest area coming up and Karin pulled in. The parking lot was crowded with cars and trucks. People milled about looking at the sky and acting agitated. Across the highway in the west-bound rest area, there were two police cars with lights flashing. Karin got out of the car and walked up to an older man who was studying the sky.

"What's going on?" she asked.

The man looked at Karin like it was an odd question. "Tornado crossed the interstate about four miles ahead."

"Tornando?" It was more of a gasp than a question.

"Touched down on the south side, jumped the road, and then came down again."

At this point Leah joined them.

"There was a tornado up ahead," Karin informed her.

"Oh my god!" Leah groaned. "What are we supposed to do?"

"Nothing to do," said the man, "but wait."

"Wait for what," asked Leah, now with a little panic in her voice. Having grown up in coastal California this was all new to her.

"Wait for the sky to stop spinning," said the man, his gaze now fixed on the clouds once more.

Karin and Leah both looked up and saw that the thick and low clouds were moving in a circular motion. It was hypnotizing in a way, frightening yet beautiful. The spell was broken by the arrival of a State Police car with lights flashing. Some people rushed up to the cruiser as the officer got out. Questions were shouted. Karin and Leah moved closer to hear whatever it was that the trooper was going to say. The man stood in front of his car and raised his hands as a gesture for everyone to calm down.

"Okay, folks, listen up," the officer shouted, but Leah noted he was smiling and confident. "The worst is over. Everyone should get back in your vehicles and wait until we open the ramp back up to the interstate. Should only be about twenty or thirty minutes."

It was then that Karin noticed another police car had blocked the exit ramp. She made eye contact with Leah and they both headed back to the car. Just as they got in it began to rain the hardest either of them had ever seen. The sound on the roof lent dramatic tympani to Karin's mood.

"This slows us down a little, but we'll be there tomorrow."

"Well, I for one will be glad," said Leah. "I have never spent this much time in a car."

Karin looked over and smiled at her sister-in-law. "You have never spent this much time outside a mall."

"True." Leah took a long moment to reflect on something more serious that was lurking in her brain. "What do you really think is going to happen when you see Meg?"

"Not sure. Well, you know I have done nothing but think about it, but there are so many possible scenarios."

"I suppose…"

Karin again swung her head to Leah. "Where did you get that 'I suppose' thing?"

"From you, dear, you use that all the time. I find it endearing."

"Hmmm. It's something my mother used all the time. We girls picked it up. It is very Wisconsin to be supposing things all the time when you reach a moment of conversational dead air."

"I suppose," Leah sing-songed, which drew a soft shoulder punch from Karin. They giggled and then suddenly the rain stopped. Karin rolled down her window. Cars were starting up.

"Looks like we can get going again," she said. "See if you can find us a place to stay in Des Moines on your smart phone."

Within a minute or two Leah had found lodging, but then Karin noticed she was pecking away in search of something else.

"What are you looking for? We can find a place to eat after we get there."

Leah nodded, but kept searching the smart phone for some information. Finally, she said, "I got it."

"Got what?" asked Karin and they finally headed down the ramp back onto the interstate. The towering clouds off to the north were now topped with orange icing from the setting sun.

"Molly Costello's phone number is actually listed in Pipe, Wisconsin."

"And?"

Leah began to dial the phone. "And I'm going to call her."

Karin looked flustered at first and then her curiosity took over. "What are you going to say?"

"I'll wing it. It's ringing."

Leah heard the metallic ring of a very old phone and then a female voice say 'hello.'

"Hello, is this Molly Costello? I see, is your mother home? Okay, well, I can call back. What? Oh, just tell her I am a friend of Roland's"

With that statement Karin's eyebrows shot into her forehead.

"My name is Leah. What is your name, dear? Sonia? Okay, Sonia, I'll call back later. Bye"

Leah ended the call and looked at Leah. "Molly's daughter."

"What did you hope to accomplish with that?" Karin asked.

"I just wanted to get things rolling. I have this feeling you are going to fold when we get to your old home town. You need me to do the bulldozing part of it, right? We have to go in like we own the place. Take over the town. Paint it red and cause a stir. Am I right?"

Karin smiled. "No, you are not right. At least not all right. You may have a role to play, but I am going to be the director."

The women were silent for a couple minutes and then Karin continued. "Actually, it may not be a bad idea to approach Meg through Molly Costello. They must know each other through the Roland connection. In fact, that was a brilliant idea, Leah."

Leah beamed. "I get one from time to time," she crowed as the car sped into the post-storm twilight of eastern Nebraska. The last light of day lit the tops of towering clouds like coral citadels on the far shores of heaven.

Sonia Costello hung up the old phone on the kitchen wall and went back to the table where she and Hector were doing homework. Hector was smiling at her as she sat down in a way that had come to thrill her. His teeth were so white in contrast with his brown face and dark hair. She loved that about him; and almost everything else now.

"Why are you smiling?'

"I like to listen to you talk." Hector nodded towards the phone.

"Why?" asked Sonia, as she twirled a curl.

"I don't know, maybe because I can hear the foreignness in your voice. Kind of like mine. It reminds me that we are not Cheeseheads."

Sonia giggled at this notion. "We live here and go to school here so therefore we *are* Cheeseheads, silly."

Hector thought that over for a second and then started to turn the pages of a text book absentmindedly. Sonia thought she had said something wrong.

"What?"

Hector raised his eyes to Sonia's where two lovely shades of brown met. "Do you ever think about your home? You know, where you were born. Your family?"

Sonia was caught off guard for a moment, but then she was already becoming aware of the serious side that Hector could offer from time to time. She admired gravity: a thing she had learned from her mother and her Papa, Roland Heinz. She stood without a word and disappeared for a minute. When she came back into the kitchen she had a magazine, which she opened and placed in front of Hector. An article had been bookmarked and Sonia opened to it. There was a two page photograph of a city of tents and crude shelters that stretched across a desolate expanse. People dressed in colorful, but shabby clothing filled in the spaces between the shelters.

"This is Darfur. This is where I came from," Sonia said and surprised herself with her tone of pride.

Hector examined the photo for a while, running his fingers over it as if to feel the sense of it. All he could say at first was 'Wow."

"I don't remember this, but I showed it to Mom and she said that I probably was born in a camp like this."

"And your mother found you?"

"No, I was taken out by a church group. My Mom got me from them. Something like that, anyway. I am Sudanese. Of course, now I am an American, but I came from this place."

Hector closed the magazine and looked at Sonia; then he touched her hand. "My home in Mexico is poor, too, but not like this." He tapped the magazine cover. "But, then poor is poor is poor. That is what my mother used to say. So we come up here and work. Some of us legal and some not, but the money goes back home so that my town will not slip into looking like your town."

"You send all your money home?" Sonia had not contemplated this before. She had little need for money on a personal level. Everything she needed was provided without question.

"We only keep money for food and rent," said Hector, but then he made a slight amendment. "Some of the men drink a little of it, too. My father says it is for the loneliness, to keep the spirits up, but I have seen them weep when they drink too much."

"That's sad, Hector."

"That is our life."

There was a long moment of fidgeting silence for Sonia. She then began to nod her head as if listening to an inner voice. Hector watched her, waiting for the next words as though he knew what they would be.

"I need to give something back to my homeland, right? Isn't that what I should do?"

"Your situation is different than mine, Sony. Your family is right here."

"Well, yes, but not all of it. What if some of my family is still there? What if they are hungry? I should do something about that."

"Maybe, but do you know how?"

Sonia was suddenly energized. "I can find out how."

At that moment Molly and Melanie came through the back door. Molly looked serious and Melanie looked angry. They had just come back from a meeting with Melanie's advisor at school. When Sonia and Hector read the body language, they exchanged looks and quick goodbyes, but not before they shared a quick kiss at the door. Sonia then followed her mother and sister into the living room where she believed a drama was about to play out.

Karin Salazar awoke in that disturbing state where she had no idea where she was. After a brief moment of panic, she figured out it was a motel room and then recognized the form of her sister-in-law sleeping in the bed between her and the window. The next thought was that she was in Iowa, only one more day's drive from her one-time home in Wisconsin and with it came another form of panic, which could not be taken lying down. She quietly got up and went into the bathroom, closed the door, and sat on top of the toilet in the dark.

It had been almost thirty years since she had run off with Jim Salazar and left Roland Heinz in her almost invisible wake. She had allowed her entire life to be erased, mostly without remorse. So why was she heading back into it? She squeezed her eyes shut making the darkness darker. Why go back? Immediately, Meg's face jumped into her mind's eye. Meg as she was back then: bitter, jealous, but still her little sister's protector. How had she handled her disappearance? Who was left of the family? What ghosts haunted The Ledge? She splashed some water in her face and went back to bed, pulling the covers up over her head. Again in total darkness, for just a minute she was the young woman she had been when last in Wisconsin. One minute later, she re-aged those three decades as she fell into a dreamless sleep in Des Moines.

CHAPTER ELEVEN

They, the birds, were always there. When I was a girl they were taken for granted partly because they flew around the sky, which was not my domain. They would catch the corner of my eye, but I did not follow them when I was young. I did not watch them with any particular wonder until later in life. Now birds are my obsession, my greatest source of wonder and delight. I now follow a flight from tree to sky, noting direction, height, and purpose. I spot them and run my brain through silhouettes, size, and colors until I can make a good guess at identity. I wish I knew all the names, but I could spend the rest of my life getting that all straight. What I think of most is an observation I read somewhere that a person would know they were in hell because there would be no birds. It comforts me daily that I walk around a place that at least has one characteristic of Heaven. And everywhere there were birds. Roland knew.

Molly stood at her bedroom window and watched the moon set into Lake Winnebago. It was 3AM and the ghosts that haunted the old farm house were up, too…and active. A front had passed through earlier and clear skies and a west wind had ridden in behind it so the newly leafed trees were swaying in the front yard, making scratching sounds against the house. It took some effort on her part to lift the warped window open a crack, but when she managed it she was rewarded with an extraordinary smell. The lake, like any big body of water had its own particular scent. Winnebago was a subtle mixture of sweet rot from the floating water plants and the freshness of water newly released from the grip of winter ice. Molly pulled a chair up to the window and sat in the moonlight and wind.

She was thinking about the conversation with Melanie that occurred a few hours ago. It had been preceded by an uncomfortable meeting with Melanie's counselor at the high school. The beer can incident had come to its inevitable fork in the road to the truth. Amber had lied about taking a drink and Melanie, knowing she lied had backed her up. Ms. Castalone seemed satisfied with the explanation that other girls were to blame and had dismissed the incident with warnings about how such bad judgment could jeopardize the girls' futures. The problem was Molly had to sit and watch her daughter lie without so much as a blink of shame. Also, she sensed that Amber and her parents were skeptical of Melanie's own innocence. Molly was still angry and conflicted as the moon dove too fast into the horizon. She told herself to let it go; that it would pass, but something still seemed to be so wrong. She heard a creak from her bed and turned to see Mel's silhouette sitting on it wrapped in a blanket.

"Sorry, Mom."

"You can't sleep either, huh?"

"I knew you were up. I hope it's not because of me."

Molly could only see the shiny black hair in the dark, not her daughter's face. The hair could pick up even the slightest light and somehow capture it. Molly thought for the millionth time how beautiful Melanie was.

"Well, you did give me something to think about today, Mel."

Melanie sighed in the dark. "Mom, I want you to listen to me, okay?"

"You have my undivided attention."

"Mom, I was put in a bad situation and I made a choice. I chose not to ruin Amber's life. If she continues to make bad choices, she will end up messing up her scholarship, but I am not going to be the one."

"Both of you could have lost your scholarships just for having beer in the room."

"So what would you have done?"

Molly heard the edge in Mel's voice. She had managed to turn the tables and her tone did not sound defensive anymore. Molly bristled.

"Okay, just tell me again that you didn't drink one drop of beer."

There was a long pause, then an arrow was launched.

"There is only one person in this house who drinks," said Melanie. "And only one."

Molly looked at the silhouette on the bed and then back out at the lake. Both were still there and not moving. There was a long exhalation. "Okay, I hear you loud and clear, honey. And I'm sorry. I have a lot on my mind right now and your little…situation threw me off balance."

Melanie stood and came over to her mother and even though they were nearly the same size now, she sat in her lap, arms around arms, head against head.

"I didn't mean it to be accusing. I only wanted to make a point. It didn't come out right."

"Oh honey, it came out just fine. You did a better job than I was doing with all this crap."

"Stinky crap."

They hugged tightly for a long moment and then Mel lofted a softer arrow. "When are you going to see Dr. Palmer? You know you want to. You guys connected somehow and he remembers you and you can't forget about him. I think it's neat. So…?"

"Babe, you may be stretching things a bit."

"Mom, listen to me. You've been acting weird for weeks…months. I know you don't sleep well. You tell us you can't write. I heard you tell Pat you have panic attacks. That's not good. You need to do something radical, something totally out of character."

"Like what, Dr, Freud?"

"Like follow your heart. Follow it to Madison."

"You've got this figured out, huh?"

"It's time, Mom. And besides…"

"Besides what?"

"Don't let Sonia land a man before you do."

Molly had to laugh, though she managed to mute it. "Hector?"

"They kiss all the time."

"No shit?"

"Yep."

"You a little jealous, Mel?"

"Hah, I could get any guy anytime, but first I get my medical degree. I not only want to be a doctor, I want to marry one."

"You've really thought this out that far ahead?"

Molly felt Melanie nod and then came another squeeze. Together they let the lake smell and the soft sound of the trees fill in the cracks of the interrupted night. Molly found she wanted to sit in Melanie's lap; the daughter being the mother of the woman. A few minutes later Mel went back to bed and Molly went to Madison in her head. She awoke the next day and found a plan had hatched beneath her pillow.

Bim Stouffer was in the garage scratching instant lottery tickets with the care of an archaeologists removing dust from a fragile artifact. It was Friday morning and this was part of his ritual for this day. So far he was luckless, especially so when his wife confronted him before he had heard her coming.

"Any luck?" asked Pat. She knew there wasn't any before she asked.

"Naw. Anyway, it's entertainment," Biff philosophized a theory even he didn't believe. So, where are you off to, Hon?"

"Molly and I are going on a road trip today to Madison."

"Oh?"

"We'll be back in time for fish fry."

"What's in Madison, if I may be so bold as to ask?"

Pat looked at her husband and shrugged. She decided to sit down for a minute and unfolded a lawn chair and pulled it up close to Bim. "You remember the guy who was attacked by the cougar over near Eldorado about a month ago?"

Bim nodded. "The guy Molly liked. Palmer."

Pat nodded and waited for the snide comment that was sure to come.

"That's pretty interesting, Honey, but it also sounds a little desperate to me."

"Desperate?"

"Yeah, desperate. Hey, she could get any guy around here with her looks and brains. So why is she going to throw herself at some guy that she only met, what, once? What you're telling me is she is either smitten or desperate."

Pat looked at Bim and drank in the man and his garage world. "Maybe she is desperately smitten, Bim."

Bim looked up from his last losing ticket and his eyes were full of honey. "Hey, I know that feeling. I had it for you,"

Pat stood up, never taking her eyes off her husband. "Had?"

"Had, do, will always."

Pat bent over and rewarded the pledge with kiss. She had originally aimed at the forehead, but changed course for the mouth. She tasted his honesty.

"Pick up some beer on the way home, Patsy."

She was walking away, but still looking at him over her shoulder. "I'll give you beer..."

Bim watched her walk away and shook his head as if in astonishment. He noticed Molly's car now at the end of the driveway and he waved at her shadow within it. He thought he saw a wave back.

"Good luck, Molly Costello," he whispered to himself as he brushed the scratch ticket dust off his lap. Somebody had to get lucky today.

Lee Krieger was working as often as he could to keep Owen's practice in Long Lake alive. When a doctor disappears for whatever reason, the clients have to move on. And so does the help, maybe. Jenny Fredericks, despite her crush on her employer was being wooed by another vet closer to where she lived in Kewaskum. Lee found her one morning apparently cleaning out her desk at the clinic in Long Lake.

"You moving on, Jen?'

Jenny was surprised by Lee's presence as he had come down the back stairs from Owen's apartment.

"You scared me, Dr. Krieger. I didn't think anyone was around." She then smiled sheepishly, shrugged her shoulders, and continued. "Yeah, I got another job offer in K-town. As you know there isn't much going on around here and I haven't been paid in a month.

Lee reached into his jacket pocket and took out an envelope and handed it to Jenny. "Here's your back pay. Actually, it's my fault it's late and I should have called you. It has been hectic lately keeping my own job going and trying to help out Dr. Palmer."

Jenny handled the envelope and then tucked it away in her purse. "How's he doing?"

"Well, pretty well, I would say. He had the first couple of surgeries to repair his face and he is being released tomorrow from University Hospital. He will be back here tomorrow night, but it will be some time before he can see patients again. You sure you want to leave now?"

"Honestly, I can't afford to stay on."

Lee looked around the small surgery where they were standing. He was trying to picture the activity; the healing and heartache that occurred there. It had all stopped on a dime. He knew Jenny wasn't deserting, just taking care of herself.

"Tell you what," he said, "You go and enjoy your new clinic. If things can get rolling again around here someday, maybe you will come back. I'm sure Owen would wish you well." He walked over to Jenny with his hand extended. She took it, one shake, and then she went out the front door. Lee locked the door behind her and walked back toward the apartment stairway. Something caught his eye. Just beneath the examining table was a gray feather with light stripes. He picked it up and tried to think of what kind of bird might have left this behind. Although he was no expert ornithologist, he was a vet and a Wisconsin outdoorsman. His first impression was a hawk, but something clicked and he was pretty sure he knew what he was spinning between his fingers.

"No, an owl," he whispered to himself. He set the feather on the table and left the room.

Molly was a nervous wreck on the drive down to Madison. Between the information provided by Melanie and some phone calls by Pat, she knew that Owen Palmer was still a patient at UW Hospital and she knew his room number. She had never fretted so much over a potted plant before, but a plant had never held the context of the one sitting on the back seat. White gardenias in a ceramic pot had gotten the nod, but only after Pat had stepped in and ended the selection process. She had told Molly that the plant didn't matter as much as the person bringing it. Molly knew she was right. She knew relaxation was the key to this visit. Actually, she knew nothing.

"What do you expect him to look like?" Pat asked. She had waited until the halfway point to pose it. Crawfish River was the point of no return.

"Melanie said his face was pretty bad," said Molly with her mind trying out different versions of bad.

"No matter what, you can't wince, Mol."

"I know...I know, Pat, but what if I do? What if he sees a flicker in my eye?"

"I got a feeling he has already seen that flicker from people. Anyway, they can fix all that stuff these days. He may end up better looking than before."

Molly gave her a 'don't press it' look. "This isn't about looks. " She paused for a full minute gathering her thoughts. "There is some sort of connection that I need to find out about. We met exactly once, but I keep thinking about him and then Mel runs into him and he told her he remembered me. Do you believe in that sort of what...fairy tale?"

"Just call me your wicked stepsister. Yeah, I believe. You can't be married to Bim and not believe in something more romantic than drinking beer in the garage."

Molly soft-punched Pat and smiled. She knew she could not do this alone.

"Thanks, Pat."

Molly noticed that the foliage in Madison was much lusher than it was seventy-five miles north in Fond du Lac. The traffic going across the isthmus and into the campus area was heavy, which added to her nervousness. It seemed like every stoplight was waiting just for her to turn red. Finally, they turned north off of University Avenue on Highland and the UW Hospital loomed on the left. Finding parking was frustrating also, but a place was finally found in the back of the garage.

Molly saw a reflection of herself in the glass door to the main lobby. She saw a stranger with a white gardenia walking into a trap. The vision was so wrong. She didn't really know the man she was seeking. She was dressed inappropriately in blue jeans and a white sweater. Her top matched the flowers, which was unthinkable. If Pat had not been next to her in that reflection, she would have turned around and driven back home and been greatly relieved doing so. The two women went through the looking glass and entered the lobby.

"You want me to wait here?" Pat asked.

It had not occurred to Molly that she would be flying solo from here on. "No, I mean, what do you think?"

"No, what do you think, Molly? This is your show."

"Yeah, my show…" Again, a quick escape entered her mind. She recognized it as a stupid and irrational thought. "I want you to come with me. It makes this all less formal."

"Okay," Pat nodded, breaking eye contact with her friend and looking for the elevators.   "There are the elevators. What's the room number again?"

"414."

Pat took Molly's arm. "Let's do it."

They entered an elevator, the last conveyance of the quest and Molly held her breath until the fourth floor pinged and the doors opened. They quickly located the directional sign for rooms and followed the hallway to the right. The door to room 414 was open. There were two beds and both of them were empty and made. There was no one in the room. Molly's eyes darted around the room, feeling let down and relieved at the same time. She set the gardenia down on the window sill, closed her eyes while shaking her head, and left the room behind a similarly dejected Pat. Molly sped past the nurses station, apparently not wanting or needing more information.

The news that he would be released that morning came as a surprise to Owen and he was unprepared. He had arranged for a ride home the next day, but now he was being turned loose in Madison without a friend or a car nearby. He did have his cell phone and an American Express card, which made everything possible, but in a somewhat delayed state. When he called Lee Krieger, he got voice mail. The same for Jenny Fredericks, although he already knew she was not his employee anymore. He decided to get a room at the hotel down the street and wait until Lee drove down the next morning to pick him up. There certainly was nothing pressing in his life right now.

Once checked in, Owen became restless. Remembering that he had left some mail at the hospital gave him an excuse to walk back down to the medical center and maybe say goodbye to the staff on second shift. He had been there for three weeks and three surgeries. There would always be part of him on 4th floor. After finding his letters still in the drawer by his former bed, he stopped by the nurse's station, finding only one RN that he knew. Her name was Betty something.

"I saw you got released, Dr. Palmer. What on earth are you doing back here?" The question was friendly and delivered with hands on hips in mock surprise.

"I left some mail, Betty. And I wanted to say goodbye and thank you."

"You were the perfect patient."

"Thanks."

"And you look a whole lot better than you did when you checked in, if I may say so."

Owen reflexively put his finger tips to his face. He knew what he looked like now, but had declined to look at the pre-op photos. The plastic surgeon had given them to him, but he just put them in a book he had been reading without a glance. The fact was he was scared to look; much like a person injured in a car accident might not want to see the car wreckage. What was the point?

"I'm sure I do."

Owen began to feel self-conscious and suddenly wanted to leave. He smiled and nodded as Betty touched his arm and gave him a sweet squeeze. He turned and headed to the elevator, but she stopped him a second later.

"Oh, Dr. Palmer, I almost forgot. Somebody left this in your room after you checked out."

Owen turned and saw the nurse holding a potted plant with white flowers. He could even smell it. Gardenias. He took the plant from Betty and caught his elevator. As the door closed he noticed a little envelope clipped to a plastic holder. In the lobby he opened it and read: *Get well, come home soon, Molly Costello.* He read the card twice and then put it in his pocket. He walked away with his fingers again mindlessly touching his new and foreign face.

CHAPTER TWELVE

It is well known that my adoptive father, Roland Heinz, and I did not spend much time together. In fact, it was only about a week. Much of that week has been documented in print by myself and others. Despite this very short time we spent together, I captured a tremendous amount of his wisdom and philosophy in interviews, kitchen table chats, and between the lines of his fabulous books. One item that stayed with me was his theory that fiction writers had unusual powers of memory. In short, he thought they never forgot anything they experienced in life. He did not think they (or him) were geniuses, but merely had all-absorbing brain sponges. He said he never forgot a thing. Not an emotional pain, a physical hurt or a childhood smell, a touch, or the angle of the sunlight when it fell upon a loved one. He let memories trigger his prose and beautify it. He said he totally lived in his mind when he wrote. Now I am beginning to suspect that the lack of that trait is my downfall as a fiction writer. I tend to block out pain. I can't or won't recall it. And yet, I sure feel it when it is happening and I have no intention of passing it on to a character in a story.

The drive back north from Madison had a strange mood for both Molly and Pat. Neither of them knew quite what to say to the other. Finally, just past Sun Prairie, Molly began to verbalize.

"What just happened today?"

Pat had been preparing her response ever since they left the hospital. "Timing is everything, Mol."

"You think?"

"And," Pat continued, "in this case it looks like we messed it up, but I hope you are not thinking of giving up? I mean, this guy is worth another try, right?"

Molly's silence was death-like. In that instant her mind decided to set her free, to let go of what she now saw as a silly, romantic notion. The idea of escaping a tricky situation was more than appealing. It bore a sense of relief she had not felt in weeks. She drew in a long breath and exhaled Owen Palmer.

"No, I mean yes, I am giving up."

"Molly, come on…"

"Pat, this was not meant to be. I just got that signal loud and clear. I was reading more into the whole thing than was ever there. I mean we only met once, for God's sake. He hugged me because I was upset that the owl freakin' died. No wonder he remembered me. I was the nut case who brought a sick bird into his office that day."

"A lot happened to him that day, Mol, but he still remembered you and mentioned it to Melanie."

"It's all bullshit. Look, don't play devil's advocate, okay? I'm fine. I get it now. I was somehow spared some real embarrassment today and I appreciate the reprieve."

"And that's how you really feel?"

"Yeah. Let's find a place to stop and get a drink. What's the next town?"

"Um, Waupun."

"Good, lots of bars there right?"

"Prison City."

"Freedom City."

In actuality, she had not left a prison and was not being freed from anything or anyone, but the cornered mind is a wily trickster and Molly was a very willing dupe at that vulnerable moment.

The directional signal went on and Molly exited highway 151 and headed into the welcoming arms of Waupun, with its main street lined with interesting choices. It was happy hour.

About ten minutes behind Molly and Pat was the SUV with California plates driven by Karin Salazar. For different reasons, but easily within a certain five degrees of connection, there was a shared nervous atmosphere as their journey came within twenty miles of ending. Leah had programmed the Holiday Inn in Fond du Lac into the GPS and the robotic female voice was the only sound besides the hum of the road beneath them. Karin broke the human silence.

"Almost there. I just want to get some food and get to bed. How are you doing, Leah?"

"I feel about the same…" A long pause and a sigh followed.

"And…?"

"Not 'and', 'but.'"

"Okay, but what?"

"'But,' I know it is going to be my job to ramrod you through this reunion so I am thinking we should try to call Molly Costello again when we get in. Maybe meet for drinks or something?"

"How about tomorrow?" Karin offered. "And you don't have to ride me about all this. Now that we are here I really want to check out my old stomping grounds and then ease into the idea of seeing my sister."

"But, you do agree, Molly is the first step?"

"I guess so. It would be good to get some inside info before just dropping from the sky on Meg."

"Okay, tomorrow, but earlier than later."

"God, you are a ramrod aren't you?"

Leah reached across and stuck her finger into Karin's ribs; more of a tickle than a jab. They both giggled as Karin's foot pressed down just a little harder on the gas pedal. Fond du Lac exits were coming up. It might as well have been Timbuktu; everything had changed over the course of all those absent years. Almost everything.

Meg Bollander had been nagged by an urge to clean house ever since she had gone under the sink and then had searched her bedroom for that book. There was a prickly feeling that she could not really identify, but it came across as a need to clean. The task was daunting. There was crap everywhere and she began by kicking things that were on the floor, as if that would help the process. She decided she needed a few large garbage bags and searched around the last place she had seen them…about a year ago. She soon discovered there were no bags, no cleaning materials of any kind. Where had they gone? The snag led to resignation that some shopping needed to be done. Her next idea led to a quickly poured Kessler's and tap water, no ice. She walked to the window with her fresh drink and looked out at the eternal view to the west. It was almost dark and there were lights on at Ghost Farm. For the first time in a long while she wondered what Molly Costello was doing, although she could not quite remember what she looked like.

Molly and Pat were sitting at the bar in The P-Town Pub. One quick one had turned into two as it was indeed happy hour. Now the bartender was wondering if number three and four would be required. Molly thought about it too long and Pat shook her head.

"We should go, Mol. I still gotta feed Bim."

"You make it sound like you have to feed your dog."

"Same thing, sort of."

Molly smiled and then lifted the last of her drink to her mouth with one hand as she twisted a strand of her hair with another. "Tell me about this Junior guy."

Pat put her emptied Old Fashioned down and swiveled her stool so she faced Molly. "You sure do flip your switches fast, girl."

"Just give me the basic information. I'm not doing anything except wondering out loud."

"Yeah, okay. Well, he's about forty-five, divorced, and really nice looking."

"What does he do?"

"He's an electrician."

"Woo hoo, sparks could fly!" Molly saw that her joke had not fazed Pat. "Sorry, couldn't resist."

"Yeah, well, maybe sparks would fly. Why don't you go out with him and see?"

"Why would he want to go out with me?"

"Well, maybe because he's seen you. Molly, he knows who you are and frankly he asked me about you."

"Oh?"

"He saw us together and then asked me if you were single."

"Where was this?"

"At Yelanek's a few weeks ago."

"Shoulda known."

"You want me to set something up? Cute guy, good job. Steady. Owns his own house out by Dotyville."

"Let me think about it. Let's get home. You gotta feed the Bimster and I should make sure the girls are eating, too."

The ladies left a couple bucks on the bar and headed out in the dusk of an incomplete day.

The local frozen custard drive-in had opened up with the arrival of the first robins and though it was a chilly evening, the carhop business was brisk. Hector had borrowed his uncle's car and Sonia was treating him and Melanie to a light supper of heavy, fried food. Melanie knew the girl who waited on them and despite her normal serenity, she was somewhat embarrassed to be seen in the back seat of an old rust bucket with her sister and her boyfriend up front. Sonia picked up the vibe.

"What's wrong, sis? "

"Nothing," said Melanie, meaning everything. "Hector, you should clean this back seat out once in a while." The remark was catty and Mel instantly regretted it. She actually liked Hector and thought that he and Sony made a neat couple.

"I don't get the car to myself enough to clean it, Melanie. Sorry."

"I'm sorry I mentioned it. Thanks, you guys for taking me out."

Sonia leaned over the seat. "How's the perch sandwich?"

"Can't taste any fish…just bread."

"Yeah, I know, but there was nothing at home and who knows when Mom and Pat are getting back?"

Mel sipped her shake, nodding as she did. "You know why they went to Madison, right?"

Sonia nodded and smiled. "Don't you just wonder what happened? I can't wait to hear."

"Hear what?" asked Hector. "What are you guys talking about?"

"Well," Sonia began, "it's a long story, but my mom sort of knew that guy who got attacked by that cougar."

"No kidding?"

"Yeah, see we had this owl and..." Sonia was cut off by a voice from the car that had just pulled in next to them. She instantly recognized the voice as belonging to Pat Stirling.

"Hey, nice car!"

Hector smiled and shook his head. Sonia frowned. Melanie waved.

Molly got out and went around to the rear window of Hector's car and knocked. Melanie lowered the glass.

"Hi Mom."

"I was just stopping to pick something up for you guys."

"We weren't sure when you would be back so here we are," said Mel.

Sonia craned over the front seat. "What happened in Madison, Mom? Did you see him?"

Molly suddenly felt like everyone in the parking lot was watching her and wondering about her day. In an instant the glow from the happy hour faded away and the evening became dark and chilly. It was a feeling she did not want to show to her daughters. She hid behind a bluff.

"Oh, well, we just missed Dr. Palmer down there. He was gone. No big deal."

The news was met with silent frowns from her daughters. She thought she understood why and reached deep for a fix.

"Hey, don't worry about me. Like I said it was no biggie. Besides, you two will be pleased to know that I am going out with Pat's friend next weekend. Okay?"

More silence. God, how they read her.

"See you at home," said Molly and walked back to her car. When she got in, her cell phone chirped. It was Melanie.

"We were just surprised to see you. Sorry about today, but that's neat that you are going out with that guy…what's his name?"

"Junior," said Molly with the word tasting bad in her mouth. She had wanted to say 'Owen.'"

"Okay….see you at home, Mom. I love you."

"You, too, Hon."

As they pulled out of the drive-in, Molly was sobbing. Finally.

CHAPTER THIRTEEN

I was recently approached by some committee woman to work on a state political campaign as a speechwriter. The word was out that my heart bled liberally and with acute feminism, so I was in demand when a young Democratic woman sought office. I found myself at a personal crossroads by this request because while I had certain leanings, I had never acted upon them. I saw traps being laid. I remember Roland and me riding back from ice fishing and the subject of politics came up. His theory was that since the Berlin Wall came down and the Soviet Union collapsed, we Americans had turned to hating ourselves depending on party lines. He said that by the time 9-11 came along, it was way too late for healing. He was wary of ever taking sides because 'to join a war without is to start a war within.' Although this political war seemed to have my instinctual backing, I could not sign on. Peace is always the goal for someone like me and doves too often drop their olive branches the day after they get elected.

When Lee Krieger arrived at the hotel to pick up Owen in the morning, he was thrown a curve by his old friend. "You want to do what?" Lee gasped.

"I called Joe Epstein over at the animal lab last night and he said it would be okay," Owen explained while really explaining nothing. "I think I need this."

Owen went on about the fact that the infamous cougar was still alive and being kept for observation at the State Animal Lab just outside of Madison and that he wanted to go see the animal.

Lee ran his fingers though his hair trying to understand the proposition. He could only come up with, "Why?"

"Look I just called Joe to find out what happened to the animal and he blew me away when he said they still had it. I sort of assumed it would be euthanized. We chatted and hung up. Then I went into the bathroom and looked into the mirror.

I saw what you see. The scars, Lee. Particularly, the pock mark where the fang broke my cheek bone. Something inside me said to go and see the animal that did this. I called Joe back and he said to come out today if I wanted to. I want to, Lee."

"You do, huh?" Lee wore a dubious look.

Owen grabbed his bag that held only pajamas, some toiletries, and a few cards and letters. It was all that was left from the day his clothes were cut off of him as he was treated immediately following the attack. Everything else he possessed was in his mind. "It is not so much that I want to go; it's more like I think I need to."

"I'm a veterinarian, like you," said Lee, "not a psychologist. Guess we all do what we need to do if we're... smart."

"Smart or not, I want to do it."

As they headed for the door, Lee spotted the gardenia. "Is this coming along?"

Owen looked at the plant and considered it. "No, it's starting to smell bad. Leave it for the maid."

It was a short drive to the animal lab.

When Molly got up the next morning, she noticed a light flashing on her answering machine in the living room. Since the land line was almost never used anymore it was a rare event to get a phone message on that line. She assumed it must be a wrong number or a solicitor of some sort. It was neither.

"Beep, Uh, hello. I am calling for Molly Costello. Hi, this is Karin Salazar. I was, um, married to Roland Heinz at one time and I am in town. Could you please call me? I would really like to talk to you. I am at the Holiday Inn, room 112. Thank you. Bye."

Molly had to replay the message to absorb the full meaning of what she had heard. "Oh my God," she whispered as she headed back into the kitchen for another cup of coffee. She found the phone number of the Holiday Inn and dialed it breathlessly. They were now connecting her to room 112. They were now connecting her to Roland's murky past and all her old instincts as a magazine writer were suddenly being fine tuned by the caffeine. Then there was a voice she never thought she would hear.

"Hello, this is Karin."

Pause. "Um, good morning. This is Molly."

The line between the two women began to sizzle.

Dr. Epstein met Owen and Lee in the parking lot at the State Animal Lab. He led them through the loading dock area and down a corridor to a room painted lime green that could only remind one of a prison movie set. The room was lined with cages, almost all empty except for two. One held a very alert and pacing wolf and the other a thin, sleeping cougar. The wolf stopped and watched as the three men walked past to the cat's cage.

"There's your friend," said Joe Epstein.

Owen took a step closer and touched the cage. He became aware of the hideous smell of an animal about to die. He had smelled it before, but never this intense. The cat had puss seeping from its closed eyes and its breathing was very shallow and ragged. There was no meat left on its bones. Owen noticed some pools of urine, but no feces. His trained eye didn't give this animal more than a day to live, if that.

"Why is she still alive? I thought she would be put down by now."

Dr. Epstein looked at Lee Krieger. He took a deep breath and turned to Owen. "I got a request when all this came down that you didn't want us to kill the cat. It was highly unusual, but then so were the circumstances. Not often a colleague and an old friend is the victim of an attack."

"I see," said Owen.

"We kept her alive at first to do some tests. See if we could find out where she came from. We also needed to observe her for various diseases. You know."

Owen nodded.

"Then we…actually I decided to let her go on for a while. Maybe I sort of knew you would want to come here," Epstein continued. "Look, I know this is not the usual procedure.

Owen, I think you and I both understand this was no mad dog. This was a beautiful creature once. It just got a little lost along the way."

"What did you find out?" Owen asked, still looking only at the cat.

"The DNA matched those other two cougars from Janesville and Chicago. Litter mates. Black Hills. God only knows why they left and came east. That's a part of the mystery we are never going to solve. She's dying fast now."

Owen turned at last and faced his friends. "What ever got them moving was also moving me into her path. If you get me the needle I would like to be the one who puts her out of her misery. That okay?"

Dr. Epstein nodded and disappeared into another room.

"Owen, why don't you let him do it?" Lee wondered out loud.

"Well, Lee, somewhere within all my delirium and dreams there were two things from all of this that I had to follow up on. Both of them female and one of them is this poor animal."

"Not sure I follow you."

Owen smiled. "Nobody follows me."

Epstein returned with the loaded syringe, handed it to Owen, and opened the cage.

Meg Bollander's legs had gone dead on her from sleeping in her chair again. She was shaky and cursing as she got up and faced her view of the lake. Only there was no lake. A thick morning fog had taken away everything outside her window. No view, no painting, she mused. Maybe today was going to be that cleaning day after all. She began to follow the concept with herself. For the first time in a couple weeks she drew a bath. Rust flew from the tap first and then cold water that wasn't getting any warmer. She quickly realized that the water heater pilot was probably out and even if she lit it, the wait for hot water would be too long in coming. With her teeth clenched and a glass of warm Kessler's set on the toilet seat, Meg lowered herself into the icy water and began to soap up. As she sipped the whiskey, she celebrated the fact that she had not induced a heart attack with her actions. In a moment or two, the water began to find room temperature and the whiskey found the pilot light in her tummy. As she soaked, she made a mental list of what she was going to need at the store. The list was short: Lysol, garbage bags, and more Kessler's.

When Owen arrived home at last in Long Lake, he asked Lee to just drop him off. He wanted to explore the clinic and his apartment alone with no outside input, no matter how kind it might be. In the clinic the first thing he found was a note from Jenny sitting on his desk. He already knew the content, but read it carefully anyway. She had worked for him for four years and he remembered the slight sexual tension between them. He wondered why he had never pursued her obvious interest in him. This train of thought brought him squarely to the last few hours he had spent there. The last few moments of his former life. He knew instinctively that the lady with the owl had been an omen, which he had failed to recognize at the time. What no one knew about Owen Palmer was that despite his education, good looks, and affable manner, he had a dark side. Anyone who dealt with animals looked so often into their eyes and actually opened them up, knew that there was another dimension to the human soul. Within that dimension lay the mystery of the other myriad of citizens of the planet earth—their mysticism and spirituality. To become a veterinarian was to join the occult world of silent eyes. Owen loved it. He loved all of them, and now most especially the soul of the cougar he had just sent away to death. The cat had whispered to him in the cage. The language of that voice had been with him since childhood. Owen knew things about animals that only humans who shared their hearts knew. The ticking of an old desk clock snapped him out of the reverie.

He spent a little time going through some business mail and quickly came to the conclusion that his practice was in its death throes. Two months away had shifted his clients to other vets that were not likely to send them back. And they were not paying their past due bills either. A small town practice was tenuous anyway. Clients came because they liked him personally. Now with the new and hideous face, they would probably stay away. Anyway, there was no way to call everyone and tell them he was back at work.

The clinic, after eight weeks of his absence, revealed its dirt and cracks, too. He had not realized how shabby the examination rooms were. The waiting and reception area was dark and still smelled of cat and dog pee. The operating suite was not clean and the time away revealed the stained metal and warped tiles on the floor. A practical voice in his head told him he was finished there. When he saw the owl feather on the instrument counter, he instantly caught the frozen moment and he thought again about Molly Costello. He was standing almost exactly, as he recalled, in the place where he had held her when the owl died. It might be time to thaw out that moment. His mind pulled up her face and for the first time, he remembered that she had a constellation of bronze flecks in her left eye. He had no idea why that came back. Then he remembered how he looked now. He came up with a quick plan, a random thought really, and then went up stairs to see if his bed was ready for his return home.

It was late in suburban Boston at the home of Harry Stompe when his cell phone sang on the table next to his favorite reading chair. An empty pre-bed snifter of brandy sat next to the phone and vibrated along with the strains of the Nokia theme song. Harry, who was now Molly's publisher, had been a long-time friend of Roland Heinz. In a way he had inherited Molly from Roland as a daughter figure along with inheriting Roland's last book, *The Needle's Eye*. The caller ID said 'Molly' and he answered it softly.

"Good evening, dear. You're calling late tonight." She could not see his smile, but heard it in his voice.

"Hi, Harry. Never too late for something interesting to pass along."

She had him hooked and Harry crossed his legs into a posture of patient comfort. "What do you have, Molly?"

"Well, Mr. Stompe, I will give you three guesses who called me tonight."

"I truly hate that game. I haven't a clue who would call you and prompt you to call me. All our mutual friends are dead and gone."

Molly cleared her throat. "Mutual friends, yes, but how about someone from the past that neither one of us has met, and yet someone we are very much connected to?"

"Still blank, Mol."

"Harry, Karin Salazar called me tonight."

There was a pause as Harry whipped through his mental roll-a-dex. "I don't know any Karin Salazar. Only Karin I can think of was…"

Molly could hear the gears mesh through the phone.

"Oh my lord," Harry gasped. "Roland's wife?"

"Bingo!"

Harry uncrossed his legs and leaned forward as if closing the distance between him and Molly. "Give it to me, Molly."

"Well, it seems she is in town to try to make some sort of amends with her sister, Meg. You remember Meg Bollander, right?"

"Of course."

"Anyway, she called me to sort of test the waters. Of course, I had to tell her that Meg has had nothing to do with me since Roland died, but that I would love to help her in any way I could."

"Have you heard from or seen Meg lately?" Harry inquired.

"I have seen her a few times from a distance. We are still neighbors, but I don't have a clue as to what she has been up to for the past five years. She's probably just sitting up in that house drinking her brains out and loathing Roland."

"She sounds like she could be quite a literary character, Molly."

Molly knew Harry was herding the conversation off in the direction of her own writing. He did have an interest in that, after all. It was his job to keep her working.

"I hear you, Harry, but no, I have not been writing any-thing lately. The fiction part of me is not alive. But, think about this; if there is another chapter in the Roland Heinz story, his ex-wife just may tell it. Might sell some of your magazines."

Harry had recently purchased *Art Harvest*, the literary magazine he used to edit. Molly's articles about the last days of Roland Heinz's life had been a smashing success in those circles years ago. A follow up article now might get the same reaction. He picked up his empty brandy glass and looked at it with disappointment. The fact was he felt like celebrating.

"Okay, Molly, dig something up. I've got tons of space to fill next quarter. Anything about Roland sells. Do you need an advance?"

"Hah! An advance? You must be interested. I'll wait and skin you when I have the story written. Deal?"

"Deal."

Okay, I'll keep you posted."

"Yes, please. Oh, and Molly, how are the girls?"

"The girls are perfect, Harry. It's Mom who is a bit shaky these days."

"Anything you want to talk about, Mol?"

"Not over the phone, but you are always so sweet to care about me."

"We should get together and talk. I'm not getting any younger, you know. Hard to get me out of my chair these days let alone travel. Maybe you'll deliver your story to me in per-son when it's done?"

"I might, but I sure wish you could come here right now. The girls would love it."

"Me, too. Let's talk some more about all of this after you meet with Karin."

"Good idea."

"Good night, Molly."

"Good night, Harry."

A thousand miles apart they both punched the red button on their cell phones and smiled at each other's faded voice echoes.

CHAPTER FOURTEEN

I was desperate to fix my insomnia so I decided to rearrange the furniture in my bedroom. Good idea, bad result. The old, high bed I had inherited from Roland had obviously never been moved since the old farmers set it there maybe seven decades ago. I wanted it by the window instead of opposite it thinking that being able to see the moon and stars (when weather permitted) would soothe me into sleep. This was something that had worked for me in my childhood in Boston. The problem was that when I moved the bed, there were things under it. I had never looked under there because of the ruffle and frankly I am not much of a house cleaner so I avoided that space. The inventory went like this: One joker and the jack of hearts from a deck of cards. Two 1937 nickels. One black checker. Six silver jacks. One squirrel hand puppet. $150 in Monopoly money and a wallet size picture of Guy Williams as Zorro. I deduced that the old farmer's kids and grandkids played under the bed. After I moved the bed, I thought I heard the kids under there at night and they were whispering to me. They knew my name.

It was another lovely spring day for garage sitting in Southeast Wisconsin and Bim Stouffer wasn't going to miss a minute of it. He had his cooler, his copy of *The Reporter*, and a radio rusting along with the pails of nails on the back shelf, was set low to a polka station. The lilacs were in full bloom now in early May and the air smelled like scented laundry softener, only better. He knew his wife was off with Molly again getting her ready for her date with that idiot Junior Bondurant, so he had the time and place to himself. Or so it seemed as he cracked open an icy can of Busch. There was somebody coming up the drive way that he didn't recognize.

Visitors were rare and mostly unwelcomed by Bim, but this guy walked with the air of someone who knew the layout of the place. There was a cockiness that translated into an ease of motion as the guy dragged his fingers across the chipped paint on the side of the house. Bim, thought maybe Pat had hired a painter. Then as the young man got closer, he saw he was no painter. He'd seen that face before on top of the china cabinet in the dining room. He'd seen a younger version of it on the door of the fridge, too. Oh shit, thought Bim, the bastard grandson has returned. In Bim's case, the bastard step-grandson, who was no doubt about to ruin his fine day.

"Hi," said Ray Hitowsky Jr. "Who are you?"

"I'm your grandmother's husband, is who I am."

"Oh, so you know me?"

Ray Jr. had a nice smile, good teeth, too, Bim noted. At least his dad's rock and roll money went for something. "I recognize your face from the wanted posters."

"You're funny. Where's grandma?"

"She's out."

Ray could now feel the hostility. He looked around the garage and yard with his eyes lingering on the old rusted swing set back by the garden. He was long removed from those days, but did feel a twinge of nostalgia. Now tall, blond, and handsome in his mid twenties, he had come back to visit his grandmother and this old coot with the beer can wasn't much of an obstacle for a kid who had done most of his growing in Beverly Hills.

"Look, mister…"

"Name's Bim Stouffer, kid."

"Okay, Bim, can we start over?" Ray walked up to Bim with his hand held out. Bim looked it over and then took it and gave it a tepid shake. The kid had guts.

"I came back here for a wedding in Sheboygan," Ray continued. "It wouldn't have been right to be so close and not visit Grandma."

Bim considered this explanation and deemed it to be legit. "You want a beer?"

Ray nodded at the offer and took an opened beer in hand, though he had no intention of drinking it. Bim gestured for him to take a seat in the folding lawn chair next to his.

"So what's that boogie woogie father of yours up to these days? Still chasing them groupies?"

Ray savored the Wisconsin accent and grinned. "Dad's slowed down a bit the last few years."

"He still playin' them stadiums out there?"

Ray smiled at the naïveté in Bim's assessment of life in the fast lane. "His health hasn't been so good lately. He mostly plays small clubs now. Acoustic stuff mostly."

"What's acoustic?"

"Guitars without amps. Just the strings. Soft stuff."

Bim took a long swallow, belched, and probed further. "So, uh, Ray...how'd you turn out? Pat don't talk too much about you. Fact is, since your mom moved to Massachusetts, it feels like we got no family anymore. What do you do?"

"Well, I've got a few things going, but mostly I sit up in my garage under the Hollywood sign and watch the world go by."

Bim's eyes narrowed as he ran his mental polygraph over this fellow. "You're shitting me, right?"

"Right."

"So, you gonna answer my question?"

"I'm in law school at Pepperdine. Should graduate next spring and then go into entertainment law."

"Hah, a lawyer. You are the devil's spawn ain't you?"

"Fuckin-A, I am."

Bim nodded his head slowly and seemed to relax. He slowly set down his beer and put his hands behind his head as if contemplating a meaningful conclusion about his step-grandson. "We could use a damned lawyer in this family. Welcome home, Ray. Your grandma will be most happy to see you. How long can you stay?"

"One night is all I got."

"Perfect."

Pat Stirling and Molly really had not been out preparing for Molly's date with Junior Bondurant. There was nothing to prepare for. Pat had set it up for Friday night and then Junior had called Molly to confirm. The big deal for today was happening at the coffee shop at the Holiday Inn as a couple stars from the cast of Roland Heinz life were meeting for the first time. The prospect of meeting Karin made Molly way more edgy than meeting Junior would be.

It was one of those summit meetings where the participants recognized each other by instinct. There were other women having breakfast at the coffee shop, but when Molly and Pat walked in they headed directly to the table occupied by Karin and Leah. Women just know this kind of thing about each other. They see searching eyes and walk to them.

"Hello, I'm Molly Costello," she said to the politely smiling ladies. "And this is my friend, Pat Stouffer."

Karin Salazar stood up as Leah remained sitting and smiling. Leah was meeting an idol of sorts and was somewhat in awe. She had read Molly's articles on Roland Heinz and also her first two novels. This was an introduction into a literary circle that she could never have foreseen.

"And I'm Karin Salazar and this is my sister-in-law, Leah Harrison."

Nods were exchanged and Karin gestured for Molly and Pat to sit.

"Thanks for coming over, Molly," Karin continued. "I was afraid this meeting might be, well, awkward."

A waitress briefly interrupted long enough to take a coffee order. No one ordered food. Pat and Leah exchanged knowing smiles. It wasn't their show and they easily assumed their roles as seconds and witnesses.

Molly, the professional interviewer, picked up the thread. "How was your trip, Karin? I know it's been a long time since you were back here. Any impressions?"

Karin had impressions as deep as the craters of the moon. "Only that absolutely everything has changed…and that is part of my reason for being here."

Molly cocked her head. They were cutting to the chase quickly.

"Molly, I know you got a part of my history with Roland from Roland. From what I have read it is all true and yet…it is not the whole story. Both of my husbands are gone now and really all I have left is Leah and my sister, Meg. You know Meg, right?"

Molly had prepared for this probe. "I know Meg, but I don't know her, Karin. We began as friends when I first came here and then when the…you know, adoption happened, she disappeared on me. Said she couldn't be my friend if I was Roland's daughter. So, yes I know Meg. I know she lives right up above me on The Ledge, but I haven't a clue as to what she has been up to for the last five years."

Karin mulled this information over. She had been hoping that Molly would be able to provide more information. "So we are both kind of out of Meg's loop?"

"I'd say so," said Molly, taking a sip of coffee.

"I drove all the way here from California to get my sister back. Do you have any interest in getting your friend back?"

"I've learned to live without her, but maybe all of this would be good for Meg. God only knows how she passes her time up there. There are very few sightings of her. But, I want something else, Karin, and you know what it is."

Karin did not look at Molly, but rather fiddled with a spoon. "You want to know my side of Roland's story, right?"

"Yes."

"To write another article?"

"Maybe."

Finally Karin's eyes came up and met Molly's. "Okay, here's the deal. You help me figure out a way to approach Meg and I will tell you my side of the story."

"For publication? On the record?"

"Well…"

"Listen, Karin, as you know, Roland still has a huge following. Anything new about his past is going to be of great interest in literary circles. I am still a writer and contributor to *Art Harvest Magazine*. It is now owned by Harry Stompe. You must remember him."

Karin nodded, still locked onto Molly.

"Look, Karin, you could just go up to Meg's door and knock and bypass me altogether. I think there is something you are not telling me and I think it is you that wants that story told. Am I right?"

It was the moment of truth. Both Leah and Pat were silently impressed by how Molly operated. Karin felt the spotlight on her, bright and hot.

She whispered now. "I came here for two reasons. One was to get my sister back and the other was to make a confession to you, Molly. A confession I have withheld for a long time. I have read your articles and there is a big lie in there. That lie is me. Let's not make this a deal, but a pact, if you get the difference. If you help me with Meg and help me with my guilt, you can write whatever you want. On the record. Everything."

At that moment Molly realized she was not dealing with a total stranger. She now recognized Roland's wife and the love of his life to be just as courageous as her husband had been. She also took a moment to appreciate how beautiful Karin was, though in her sixties. In Molly's mind this was not some battered wife who just ran away, but rather a complex woman with a sense of family and justice.

"Let's take this a step at a time, okay?" said Molly. "We need to bring your sister into this circle."

"Do you have any ideas, Molly?"

"Something is hatching."

Without thinking about it, Molly reached over and put her hand on top of Karin's. It was warm and it turned on the table to grasp Molly's. The Holiday Inn summit had reached an accord.

When Molly dropped Pat off at the end of the driveway she couldn't resist a comment on Bim's lifestyle.

"Does he sleep out there, Pat?"

Pat got out of the car, but leaned back in. "It sure seems like it, but I am not sure that you've noticed that we passed at least a dozen garage sitters just coming across town. It's a Wisconsin male, cultural thing, I guess."

"You think Junior is a garage sitter?" Molly asked, only half joking.

"You are sure going to find out on Friday. Bye, Mol."

"Yeah, bye."

As Molly pulled away, Pat noticed that there was some-one sitting with Bim. A few steps later she recognized her grandson and a light came on inside her. Not only was Ray Jr. home, but he was apparently coexisting with her husband. She was already thinking about ways to celebrate these great things.

Molly, upon returning to Ghost Farm was making other calculations. The concept of bringing Meg Bollander and her sister together was stimulating her imagination. She felt the need to take one of her long walks and think it all out. She fig-ured the magazine article that would ensue was the easy part of the equation. That would be the ending. It was the begin-ning that was problematic. How could she draw Meg out of her seclusion without forcing her out and into an awkward sit-uation that might collapse this house of many cards? A walk around the perimeter of her property usually solved most problems. Half way through her walk, the solution presented itself in a most profound way. She wondered why she had never thought about it before. It just might work. She was so pleased with the idea that she decided to cross-cut the walk and head directly back home. Then she thought of Junior Bondurant and finished the four mile hike. One problem was perhaps solved, but one other one loomed. Friday was three days off. Three too many days and three too few.

CHAPTER FIFTEEN

So what goes on when you're dead? Once again I have to reference my adoptive father, Roland Heinz, because if he is my guide then I am ready for the world to come. If I am true to him and my own heart then Heaven is revealed by opening the curtains in my bedroom in the morning. I face west to the inland sea of Winnebago. Heaven, it seems, has a couple water towers, some wind turbines, and often a morning gloom that is hard to cut. But, then Heaven began long ago with my parents' love and then began to change its shape and color as I grew from a fertilized egg into…me. Oh shit, I am still so Irish Catholic Boston, but still I live and breathe in Wisconsin now. Maybe I died on the flight here from Logan to Mitchell. If so, I do indeed rest in peace…unless I am only dreaming of Heaven. Why does it matter so? And jah. And hey.

Day break at Long Lake was always awesome for Owen Palmer. His bedroom window on the second floor of his office/apartment faced east and the whole tableau of dawn in the Kettle Moraine was his daily rebirth. He did the coffee ritual and for the first time in many days he checked his email while blackbirds gabbled outside his window. It was not lost upon him that their indifferent language was somehow digitalized and splattered across this computer screen. He wondered how he could be gone so long and no one really noticed. He had no immediate family anymore. There were a couple of solidarity notes from colleagues and friends, but nothing of substance. Substance; a good word for a man about to turn fifty and knowing that the previous half century had just been wiped out by a lost wild animal.

His practice was gone to hell and his face was remade into a mask that had inherited a bitter twist. He tried to see past the scar tissue and find his old self. It was there somewhere. The moment of self-pity made him sentimental and he looked inside himself for a fix. The late spring dawn over the mists of Long Lake was a sort of survivor's trigger and it came with the first sun ray through the trees on the far shore. He discovered that morning that the stranger in the mirror was not so strange. The cat had dragged him away from being handsome to being rugged. Vanity. Maybe it would work. He went to the bathroom sink and drew ice cold and hard Long Lake water into the sink. He took a fresh bar of soap out of the box and eventually made lather, which he scrubbed into his face as if he were trying to clean his soul beneath the surface. There were places that hurt still, but he dug into them extra hard. He rinsed and he toweled. And then, as if the towel was a mummy's wrapping, he revealed himself to himself. Fierce eyes looked back in the mirror. He could pass as human...maybe. He decided instantly to try the new Owen out on Jenny. A sort of testosterone test. He thought she might be glad for the attention after putting her off for so long. After he dialed her number and brought the cell phone to his face, he quickly changed his mind and closed it. There was just the slightest hint of gardenia, perhaps from the soap on his hands and, after a long moment of contemplation, he knew what he had to do. It wasn't the first time he had assigned some sort of vague feelings to the owl woman, but it was the first time they had crystallized.

Karin Salazar and Leah Harrison spent their morning driving around Fond du Lac, as they had for the past four days. They had parked on Main Street and walked up and down, marveling at the shops that seemed to be stuck somewhere in past decades. Time did freeze in small towns that still had main streets. Leah, who had never been to this part of the Midwest before was more impressed than Karin. Karin had hoped the town had gone through some major changes since her departure, but change was on the outskirts of town. Main Street was the same.

"Actually, these wedding dresses are lovely...in quaint way," Leah observed as they stood in front of a bridal shop window display. "The mannequins still have faces here."

Leah noticed that her sister-in-law was not listening. Or maybe she was just tuning her out.

"Karin, did I say something wrong?"

Karin turned away from the window and faced the street. A sigh and a second later, she spun back to Leah. "I bought my wedding dress here. The first one."

"Oh, I'm sorry…"

"The store had a different name back then, but the mannequins…those are the same. It's a kind of sharp stab from the past. I hadn't expected that kind of reaction."

Leah took Karin by the arm. "Okay, babe, let's keep moving." And they did until they were standing in front of a small, locally owned bookstore. In that window sat the other half of Karin's first wedding memory. *The Needle's Eye* in soft cover was displayed in a little pyramid. Next to them was a photo of Roland in a frame. Beneath the frame was a hand-written sign that read, 'Hometown Author, Roland Heinz." Both women stared at the display, but with different thoughts and reactions.

Leah thought, 'Wow, I'm in my literary idol's hometown.' Karin thought, 'Oh my God, what was I thinking coming back here.' They turned and faced each other, reading faces, not books.

"You got that look again," said Leah.

"No shit."

"You can't turn away from a place you've already arrived at."

Karin gave a pained look, but she knew Leah was right.

Leah continued, "And Saturday night is the big reunion with your sister. You do want that, right?"

"Yes, but the big reunion could be a big mess."

Leah realized that she may have been enjoying all of this drama just a bit too much, but charged through her brief moment of guilt. She once again took Karin by the arm and led her away from the bookstore. "Where are your *cojones*, Karin baby?"

"Same place yours are, Leah baby."

"Missing since birth!" they both said at the same time, which prompted the laughter needed to get back on track. They decided a supper club in the Holyland would finish off the day.

Friday finally arrived at Ghost Farm and the weekend was going to be so busy that Molly was fumbling through post-it notes as not to miss any details.

"Hey, you two," said Molly to Sonia and Hector, who were lounging on the sofa like it was Cleopatra's barge on the Nile. Sonia held the TV remote like a scepter and tortilla chips and salsa were on the coffee table looking ravaged.

"What Mom?"

"Every time I come home you guys are watching TV as if there were nothing else in the world that matters. Hi, Hector."

His Latin smile lit the room making Molly feel like a scold. She liked this kid, but seeing him and Sony entwined on the couch was always disturbing. She knew it was mostly just a love-envy thing and returned his blinding smile with one of her own.

"I have a project for you two. Do you think you can turn off whatever crap you are not watching and help me?"

Hector stood up politely. "What can we do, Mrs. Costello?"

Molly couldn't resist the correction. "It's not Mrs. Costello because there is no mister Costello. And Hector, you can just call me Molly because, well just because, okay?"

"Okay,"

"Sony, you know the place where the wind turbine used to be?"

"Yeah, Mom."

"Can you guys go around and pick up all the branches that blew down over the winter and take them over there. You know, anything that will burn."

Sonia was intrigued. "Yes we can do that, but why?"

Molly was glad the question was being asked, but there was a mystery to it all that she wanted to draw out. "Just do it and I'll tell you later."

"No, Mom, now." said Sonia.

"You don't need to know everything now, honey."

At this point Hector took the role of moderator. "No, Sonia, we should just do what your mother asks with no questions."

Sonia gave Hector a look that he had not seen before. He was taking sides and while he wasn't

on the wrong side, he was pushing it. She felt a small sense of betrayal. Hector recognized that he had wandered into the land between mother and daughter and retreated. "We can help, right Sonia?"

Hearing him say her name again so sweetly allowed Sonia to relax her shoulders and nod to her mother. It was a subtle moment that Molly understood, but she was amazed that this thing happened so young in life; this family pecking order. She decided to give more information. "We are making a bonfire for Meg Bollander."

That made Sonia's eyebrows leap an inch. "Mrs. Bollander?"

"See, this is why I didn't want to explain the whole thing...but I will...a little."

Molly sat on the coffee table opposite the couch and idly loaded a chip with salsa. "Meg's sister is in town and we are going to arrange a meeting between them."

Sonia started to explode into another question that Molly defused. "They haven't spoken to each other in a long, long time, honey. We are going to create a...situation...a bonfire to lure Meg."

"What time is your date coming, Mom?" Melanie asked as she peeked into the bathroom as Molly applied her eye makeup. She had used a tone that Molly wasn't used to.

"He's picking me up at seven. That okay with you, Mel?"

"Well sure. You look...nice, Mom." Same tone.

"Okay, what's wrong with how I'm dressed?"

Melanie slipped into the bathroom and took a seat on the toilet lid. "Are you sure you want to wear jeans on your first date?"

Molly smiled into the mirror. "We are going to a bar for dinner and drinks. A place out in the Kettle. I think these jeans are dressy enough. At least they don't have a bib front or hammer loops."

"He's taking you to a bar?"

"It's not what you think, Mel. It's a nice place, kind of rustic, I hear. Good food. Besides, I may need a drink after I meet this guy." Molly checked her makeup and put the eye shadow brush down. She turned to her daughter looking cheerier than she felt. "Blind dates are weird. Avoid them at all costs, okay?"

"Don't worry."

"I rarely worry about you…"

"Where's Sony?"

"She and Hector are doing some work for me."

"Oh?"

"Yes. Listen, dear, tomorrow night we are having guests. Two ladies from California. One of them is Mrs. Bollander's sister and I am trying to get Meg to come down and talk with her."

"I don't get it. Why wouldn't they just go ring Mrs. Bollander's doorbell if they want to see her?"

"It's complicated, okay? I've gotta run. Junior will be here any minute."

"Junior?"

"I'll tell you all about everything tomorrow. Bye" Molly made for the stairs with Melanie right behind her.

"Mom, you can tell me tonight when you get home. I'll wait up."

"Don't you dare."

Just then the buzzer at the back door signaled Junior Bondurant's arrival. Three long buzzes.

Sonia and Hector inspected their gathered pile of branches as they held hands and watched the sun dropped down into Lake Winnebago.

"So, there used to be a wind turbine here?" asked Hector.

"Yep, but my Papa Roland had it taken down."

"Why in the world would he do that, Sonia?"

Sonia looked at Hector and the two brownest sets of eyes in the county met. "I'm not exactly sure. It had something to do with the lady who lives up there." She pointed to Meg Bollander's farm, looming above them on The Ledge.

CHAPTER SIXTEEN

I think I felt it today—the spontaneous guilt of being human. I was driving in my new Subaru Forester on Highway 151 between Pipe and Calumetville and it was a busy morning. I was trying to finish up a cell phone call to my sister in Boston while eating a Danish, and listening to NPR. I was distracted and absorbed in the twenty-first century ritual of multitasking and micro-managing. My brain scarcely knew which cell to fire when and what for. I felt digital. And then out of nowhere my eye caught motion on the right side of the road. In an instant that will be singed onto the retina of my eye and the photo paper of my brain there arose a flying specter. They don't take flight often, but this wild turkey may have been so infuriated by my buzzing techno-presence that it flew up and aimed itself toward my windshield. In an instant so rare that it snatched my attention, the big bird flew inches away from me and looked directly at me with a wild eye that could not hide its disdain. I flinched and ducked, but the instant passed. But, then it will never pass. The message of the turkey eye was right; I am an intruder, an outlander on a planet I will never understand. There is no lower species: no minor soul unlit.

Ray Hitowski Jr. sat at Pat's kitchen table eating a brownie just as he had done more than a decade ago. He had always felt safe at Grandma's house, especially back in the days when his parents were fighting their distant war. Grandma never took sides and he liked that even though he knew that his mom had her ear all the time and his dad was far away. Now his father was on one coast and his mother was on the other. Ray pondered the fact that he was now seated at the fulcrum of a family scale that was somehow balanced, even if it no longer mattered.

"What are you thinking about, Ray? You look a million miles away," said Pat.

Ray refocused himself to the familiar surroundings and found his Grandma's eyes. He lit up his best smile. "I was thinking about when I was a kid. I always loved this house, Grandma."

"Well, this old house was always the common denominator, isn't it? Not much has changed, huh?"

"Except for Bim, right?"

"What do you think of him, honey?"

"He's a bit crusty, but I like him. He's good to you, right?"

Pat poured herself a cup of fresh coffee while she phrased her response. When she turned back to Ray she was smiling warmly. "Yeah, he's good to me. And he's good for me, too. Loneliness is an awful state in which to live. He is a good man and we get along just fine."

"Do you ever think about Grandpa?"

"Well, sure I do, but never when Bim is in the room. It works that way."

"I suppose."

Pat sat down at the kitchen table across from Ray. Now it was her turn. "Okay, hot shot, you got a woman in your life out there?"

Ray knew this was coming. He had just answered the question a dozen times from friends at the wedding in Sheboygan. "No one special, Grandma."

"You date around, huh?"

"A little."

"Not like your old man, I hope."

"Grandma, Dad's reputation is about all he has left of the old him. He's been with the same woman for years. Her name is Marcia and she's a nurse. They live in a bungalow in Pacific Palisades and almost never leave the house. I mean to go out and party. I think he's writing a book or something about his glory days."

"Oh lord, I hope he keeps your mom out of it."

"You know what, Grandma, Dad never, ever knocks Mom. He used to when I was first out there, but after the divorce, he speaks very kindly of her. How is she, anyway? You hear from her much?"

Pat took a long sip of coffee. Her daughter, Carrie, was still her pride and joy. "We talk all the time, though I don't see her too often. She's doing just fine out in Massachusetts."

"What's she doing out there? I mean, I know she lives with Mike Gabler."

"She pretty much runs the business end of his photography studio. He made her a full partner, and as you know, he makes quite a bit of money."

"I guess. You think they are ever going to get married?"

"That's hard to say. I think she is still leery of taking that leap after being married and abandoned once before."

That thought made Ray wince a little. He knew he was the very bone of contention that caused the bad marriage of his parents. Pat read his mind.

"It was my fault all that happened back then, Ray. I was the one who insisted they get hitched when you came along. Don't blame anyone but yours truly, for what happened before."

"I don't blame anyone, Grandma. Life is tricky."

Pat nodded in agreement. She was proud of how Ray had turned out despite his early days, but a change of subject was badly needed. "You're coming out to supper with us tonight, right?"

"Don't tell me. Fish at Yelanek's?"

"Of course, it's Friday night in Wisconsin, right?"

"Friday and fish. Something's never change."

"Well, that one doesn't. Listen, Bim hates that place, so he won't be coming, but I am taking my friend Molly's girls out tonight. Molly has a big blind date that I sort of arranged so I got the kids. It'll be fun."

"Molly is the writer, right?"

"Right. The one Roland Heinz adopted before he passed. She's my best friend."

"She's a lucky lady to have that title, Grandma."

"Hah, we're both lucky. Come on with me and I'll show you your room and get you some towels. We leave here in about an hour."

Ray knew where his room was and knew where the towels were kept, but he followed Pat up the stairs just as he did when he was a little boy. He took one step back in time for each step up to the second floor of the house that represented peace to him. He counted the steps. The seventh one should squeak. It did.

Molly opened the back door and hit the porch light simultaneously. Her first impression of Junior Bondurant was something like, oh my God, the man is gorgeous! Junior was about six feet four, dark curly hair, blue eyed, and built like a lumberjack. He was dressed like one, too: jeans, flannel shirt, with a tan leather vest. Molly was smiling like a little girl opening up a Christmas present.

"Hi, you must be Junior. Come on in." She held the door for him as he stepped into the kitchen.

"And you must be Molly." The voice was soft and deep. "Only I don't go by Junior. Everyone just calls me JB."

"Okay." Molly was already twirling her hair. This dose of male beauty was making her stupid.

"I gotta tell you, Molly, you look beautiful. Thanks for going out with me."

JB was saying all the right things and Molly's walls were coming down a minute into her date. She quickly yelled goodbye to Melanie, knowing Pat would be picking her and Sonia up for dinner soon and wanted to make a hasty escape before Pat arrived. In the driveway she was confronted with the biggest pickup truck she had ever seen. It was black and chrome with *Bondurant Electrical* and a lightning bolt stenciled on the door. She walked around to the passenger side and waited for JB to open the door for her, but he was already in the driver's seat. She heard the click of the door unlocking and climbed up into the cab. She let the lapse in courtesy pass. She wondered briefly if any men opened doors for women these days.

The interior of the truck was spacious and very clean. There was a hint of some scent that she thought might be testosterone. When JB started the engine, she could feel its power through her feet and butt. It thrilled her. Molly felt like a teenager going to the prom with her dreamboat. She smiled like a lunatic in the dark. She quickly deduced he was the strong and very silent type.

"So how's the electrical business these days?" Molly asked. It sounded dumb to her, but they had driven a couple miles and he wasn't saying a word. She chose work over weather as an icebreaker.

"It's okay, but I don't want to talk about work tonight, Molly."

"I didn't think you were going to talk about anything," She giggled.

"Tell me about yourself," he said. "Tell me what you do for fun around here."

Fun. That one threw Molly for a moment. Why did this guy have to ask such a hard question first? She decided to bend the response. "I guess I write for fun."

"Oh yeah, that's what you do. You're a bookwriter."

That term threw her again. It sounded a tad rustic. "I write novels. Do you read much, JB?" It was a question that she thought she already knew the answer to.

"Hah, I read all the time. *Outdoor Life, Field and Stream. Gun Magazine*, too."

"I see." He didn't read.

"I ain't got no time for books; just magazine articles mostly. Electricians are on call 24/7, you know."

She didn't know that fact, but as she looked at his profile, lit by the dashboard lights, she cut him miles of slack. He was absolutely gorgeous. Besides, she thought, it wasn't a night for boring literary musings. It was a night for fun.

When they pulled off Route 45 and headed into the Kettle Moraine, Molly was not paying much attention to where they were, but something made her come aware as they stopped at a stop sign at the intersection of County's SS and G. Across the road was a sign proclaiming *The Jersey Flats Prairie Development Project*. The headlights briefly lit a bird painted on the sign. She'd been at this crossroads once or twice before. The memory was only subliminal at first, but there was flash of a rock formation with trees that stood somewhere out in the darkness. The vision was gone as fast as it came, and a minute later, they were at the fish fry bar in New Prospect where cars were parked up and down the road.

"This place must be good. Looks popular," Molly said.

"Yah, anyplace with good perch is popular on Friday night. I come here because it's out of town and the lawyers, politicians, and other shitheads don't wander out this far."

The real JB was beginning to emerge, Molly thought, but this time he came around and helped her down from the truck. His strength and overall hunkiness did a mind wipe on his words.

Inside was a sort of controlled bedlam. The place was packed. They got on the list for a table, but were told it might be about an hour wait. They went to the bar where someone had just gotten up leaving one seat. JB made Molly sit while he stood over her like a mantling raptor. She didn't mind at all. She ordered an Old Fashioned and he had a beer. Two drinks later, a stool opened up next to Molly and JB grabbed it. He slipped his arm over the back of Molly's stool and leaned into her.

"I had no idea we were going to have to wait so long. You wanna go somewhere else?"

"No, this is okay. I don't mind waiting."

"You want another drink?"

Molly was already feeling pretty good after two and against her better judgment she nodded. It was that third Old Fashion that turned the corner so subtly on the night and she began to free fall into JB's penetrating eyes. By the time a table was available, neither one of them wanted to eat. By the time Old Fashioned number four arrived, Molly had her hand on JB's thigh and he was rubbing her shoulder with his strong right hand. The blind date that had started out so quiet had been totally drowned out by their loud screaming of hormones.

Ray Hitowski Jr. had barely paid any attention to Sonia and Melanie when they had hopped into the back seat of his

Grandma's minivan. Pat did all the introductions and mostly talked to the girls, teasing about their mom's blind date. When they got to Yelanek's Supper Club in Jericho, Pat asked him to jump out and get on the waiting list, which he did. A few minutes later when Pat and the girls walked up, he got his first real glance at Sonia and his first very amazing look at Melanie. And vice versa. Somewhere in the cosmos two streaks of primordial lightning ignited and crashed into one another. The thunder was immediate. Mel was the most beautiful female he had ever seen. Ray was the handsomest man Mel had ever encountered. They quickly gauged ages, intelligence, and chemistry and were dumbstruck sorting it all out. Pat noticed. How couldn't she? The smell of electrical fire overwhelmed the smell of cigarettes, fish, and beer, which was no easy task.

During supper Sonia kept Pat from eavesdropping too much into Ray and Mel's getting-to-know-you conversation. They were lost in it, anyway: tuning out the crowded room and the rest of the world, for that matter. Their eye contact was only broken by the waitress, who brought huge plates of fish, fries, and coleslaw that neither one of them would eat. At one point, Pat leaned into Sony and whispered in her ear.

"What do you make of those two?"

"What?" Sonia looked around and then realized that Pat was talking about the other two people at their table. "Oh, yeah, she likes him."

"Likes? They haven't taken their eyes off each other all night."

"Yeah, well it's about time."

"Huh?"

"She is too pretty to be little miss doctor all the time. She says she is not looking for a boyfriend, but she is and tonight she found one she likes."

Pat was thinking about their age difference, but another fact trumped that. "Sonia, Ray is going back to California tomorrow."

Sonia locked her big brown eyes on Pat and shook her head. "He isn't going anywhere tomorrow, Pat."

Just then Pat's cell phone rang. The caller ID announced Molly.

"Hi Mol, what's up?"

"Pat, I need to ask you a question." Molly was calling from the lady's room at the bar in New Prospect.

"Geez, Molly, you sound…drunk." She had whispered the last word.

"Yeah, about half in the bag. Listen, can you take the girls home with you tonight?" The question dangled in cellular air for a long moment.

"Things are going that well, huh?" Pat was trying not to let Sonia in on the gist of the call.

"I don't know…I guess. I just want the coast clear in case…"

"Okay, okay, I get it. I need to call Bim real quick and get him prepared, but I guess it is okay."

"Thanks, Pat. Talk to you tomorrow, okay?"

"Sure, have fun." Then Pat thought of something else. "Hey Molly…"

"Yeah?"

"You're not the only one having fun tonight. My grandson and your oldest."

"No shit?"

"Yep. Talk to you later. And be careful, huh?"

Molly was still trying to imagine Melanie being interested in Pat's grandson. She had to search her mind for his name and came up empty. The drinks were up there now. She closed her phone and checked herself out in the mirror. "Molly, you little slut," she whispered.

CHAPTER SEVENTEEN

Damn writer's block. Maybe the only way to break it is to write an article entitled '1000 Excuses Not to Write'. Roland always said it was mind over matter; that the brain was full of baby words waiting to be born. That was pure Roland. Pure Molly's brain is empty this morning, as per usual lately. I took my coffee and walked out to the cheese shed studio and pulled up an afghan and my laptop. What showed up on the screen was this: Dear God, whisper in my ear. Tell me a story of your silent life and I will tell it to the world. Use me to entertain and to heal; even if it is just one lonely person sitting home sick with just a book for a friend. My gift from you requires one of your lightning bolts from time to time. I then sat back and waited for far off thunder. I was totally startled when I heard it coming across the lake.

Owen Palmer was committing the ultimate sin of a Friday night in Wisconsin. He was at home alone, sober, eating meat, and reading a book. He had thought about going out. There was a fish fry bar that he had gone to many times just down the road in New Prospect, but he was not quite ready to be *not* recognized by some familiar faces. He rarely drank, anyway, so he decided not to be social at all. The meat was a couple of nuked cheeseburgers that were only slightly better than hospital food and required no preparation. The book was entitled, *Silent Silos* by Molly Costello. Dr. Palmer was spending this Friday night getting to know Molly. He read this passage twice:

The silent towers that held the grain and hope of departed generations are now their tombstones, scattered across the rolling hills like abandoned Norman keeps, sagging and decaying in the spring wind. They survive only as aviaries and shadow-casters; sundials whenever there is sun. They breathe melancholy from their turrets, accessible only by rusted rungs that no one would dare climb. And at the bottom of each old silo is a doorway. I haven't the courage to enter one, but I think if I did I would find the wormhole to another world where spiders weave dreams around granary mice and smiling snakes.

Owen closed the book, but not before spending a long moment staring at the author's photo on the inside back of the dust cover. The snake reference made him smile as he recalled a confrontation between a red racer and gardener when he was visiting an aunt down south as a child. He remembered an image like a smile on that snake. He hadn't thought about it in years. Writers could do that to you, he thought. He had never really known an author. People who could fit words together like she could were rare. They had an inner vision. He thought his scientific mind might benefit from getting to know her better. That is what he told himself, but deep down he knew it was not science wanting to meet literature. He had sensed that fateful day in his office that she had stepped inside his well guarded perimeter and was on her way to his heart. Inside that perimeter, the cougar still hunted and a hundred castrated black labs and golden retrievers still sired pups. He had that thought and then tossed the book aside, as though chiding himself for such foolish thoughts. He threw his feet up on the couch, laid his head on a pillow, and stared at the ceiling. He wondered why any of this fantasy mattered. Perhaps his wounds had made him crazy. Maybe he was longing for something, anything that happened before the cat jumped him. Had Molly Costello really happened to him? The ceiling had no clue.

There was slip of paper on the coffee table with a phone number in Pipe. He had looked it up about a week ago, but could not summon the courage to dial it. He had tried practicing his lines: *Hi, I wanted to thank you for the gardenia. My face is a mess and my skin grafts are weeping, but maybe we could meet for coffee or something?* There were a hundred variations on this theme; none stood the light of recitation. But then, when there is no other solution one must do the obvious. He sat up and grabbed the slip of paper and his cell phone. Owen wondered what she was doing at that moment as he forced his fingers to punch out her number. It rang and he squeezed the phone so he wouldn't drop it.

What Molly was doing at that moment was getting aroused. JB's truck was speeding back up Rt. 45 toward Fond du Lac and the intersection of Hwy 151 to Pipe. She had let him paw her a little in the parking lot and they had shared a kiss that was powered by alcohol. Although she was more than tipsy, she was being coldly logical in dealing with her desire. She told herself she didn't care if she was his piece of meat for the night. He would be hers, too. It had been so long since she had been with a man that it would be like going back to sex school. She owed it to herself after being cooped up at Ghost Farm like it was some sort of self-imposed nunnery. His hand was back on her leg as though assuring her that her thoughts were legitimate. She turned and looked out the window and saw her own smile lit by some passing yard light. I am in control, she thought. I'll use this stud and send him on his way. We have nothing to talk about, but then I don't want to do any more talking. Her ears were hot and humming. Soon they were heading up her driveway. The porch light was on, but there were no other signs of life. As she got out of the truck and fumbled with her keys, her only thought was whether the playground would be the couch or her bed.

Everyone had gone to bed at the Stouffer house except Ray and Melanie, who were at the kitchen table eating ice cream. Even the garage sitter was upstairs, leaving the house quiet and intimate. These were the moments following instant attraction where everything else was sorted out. Some of it was practical and some of it was a mixture of posturing, preening, courtship and outright lying.

"Well, I love the medical program at UW, but I really would have liked some more choices in other parts of the country," said Melanie trying to sound worldly. She was even putting a little worldly affectation into her voice. "I know there are some good med schools in California."

Ray considered this statement, but what he was really wondering was how old this amazing person was. Age is important or maybe not so much. "You said you are leaving high school early?"

Mel let her spoon linger in her mouth. She knew the information he wanted and it provoked her. "Yeah, Ray, I'm a smart kid...and I'm seventeen. So, how old are you? How much money do you have? Are you straight or gay? Liberal or Conservative?"

Ray put his palm up in protest. He back lit it with a smile. "Whoa, I get it." What he got was that she was seventeen and smart. He decided to cut to the chase. There was a plane reservation to either meet or cancel. "Melanie, we are sitting here talking because we...you know, liked each other immediately, right? The real question is what are we going to do about it?"

She couldn't help noticing how much he looked like his mother. He had Carrie's eyes. "Keep going." She was bracing for some sort of weird proposition.

"We can either..." Ray thought he knew where he was heading, but Melanie's big, gorgeous Asian eyes were unraveling his thought process. It was late. Without any conscious forethought he nudged his chair back with a squawk on the waxed floor and stood up. He walked around the table and held his hand out. Melanie stood up like a woman who had been asked to dance at a cotillion. In the most special instant of her life, she let him take her into his arms. For the next three minutes, all they did was hug silently and rock. It was the sweetest thing that had ever happened to Melanie. It was the clearest message she had ever gotten from a boy or man.

Sometime during minute number three, Bim showed up in a shabby terrycloth bathrobe. "Looks like you kids hit it off, huh?" Everybody smiled, nobody meant it.

At Ghost Farm it was the couch. Molly had opened a bottle of wine that was a total waste because she was already drunk, loosened up, and ready for JB. He had no interest in an amusing little Zinfandel at this point in the evening either. The house was quiet and dark, except for the floor lamp at the end of the couch where JB sat looking confident and comfortable. Molly was perched on the coffee table, staring at him and admiring her conquistador in the soft light.

"Com'ere once," JB said and held his hand out to her. Molly held her ground for the expected count of three and then came there once. In a motion that was both clumsy and ballet-like, Molly launched herself on top of JB and they began the preamble to sex. His hands were first outside the back of her jeans and then inside them. Molly was operating on pure instinct now, but there was an unexpected gesture of modesty as she reached up for the little metal chain that controlled the lamp. Pulling that chain was going to be her last act of surrender after almost seven years of abstinence. She jerked it hard and then there was a loud pop. The light went off, but it apparently blew every fuse in the house. She could hear the refrigerator groan and come to a halt in the kitchen. Outside the yard light went out, too, leaving the whole property in blackness that only the blind could know.

"We blew a fuse," whispered Molly.

"Yeah, I'm about to blow something, too," said JB. He was beyond caring about lighting or cooling.

Molly tensed up and tried to see in the dark. The fact that she could not see anything made her panic. She rolled off of JB and fell on the floor. "I can't see a freaking thing!"

JB's arms were flailing for her. "We don't need to see nothing."

Molly blinked and squinted. She listened for the wind up clocks and each of them tick-tocked almost too loudly in the darkness. She found the coffee table with her hand and sat on it again, amazed still that there was not one single photon of light in the house. It frightened her and also seemed to sober her.

"Do something," she said,

"Do fucking what?"

"You're the electrician for cry-eye! I've got food in that fridge that's going to spoil!" She heard the panic in her voice and tried to disguise it. "JB, please. I hate this total darkness."

She heard and felt him sit up across from her. "Okay, where's the fuse box?"

"It's in the basement."

She saw the flicker of a very small light come on in his hand. Of course, the electrician would have a tiny flashlight. He sighed and swore, but she knew he was moving. "How do I get down there?"

"The door is in the kitchen on the left when you go in."

JB's tiny light moved away from Molly and headed into the kitchen leaving her feeling stupid. She knew she had ended the night's extracurricular activities by blowing that fuse, but somehow there seemed to be no remorse. If JB was going to be her sexual savior, he'd have to be willing to take her out again. The idea was trying to soothe the realization that she had almost yielded to this guy on the first date, which was something her mom had always preached against. It was still dark and girlhood rules and promises were flashing in her brain. Then she heard the appliances come back to life, including a loud beep from the answering machine. She heard JB's feet on the basement stairs. She tried the floor lamp, but the bulb was blown. She got up and groped for the kitchen and found the light switch. Reality was blinding.

The man that emerged from the basement was still gorgeous, but the mood was gone for the night. He looked at her and knew it too when he made one step toward her and she took one step back.

"I guess that fuse blew everything, huh?" JB said.

Molly nodded. "I'm sorry."

JB gave her a long look, hard and penetrating in its implications. "Yeah, so I'll call you."

"Okay." It was a neutral word.

Although they had been on the brink of intimacy a few minutes before, he left her without so much as a peck on the cheek. Molly watched as he went out the back door and she didn't move until she heard the roar of the truck's ignition and liftoff. Suddenly she was both drunk again and tired. It was a long climb up to her bed and she got into it without undressing. Friday's expectations were now ending in Saturday's oblivion. No tears, just a black nothing. But, then there was something that made her eyes pop open. The answering machine! What if it was the girls and something was wrong. No, they would have called her cell phone, she reasoned. Molly grabbed the pillow and hugged it tight, trying to nod away, but the sound of that machine beeping kept coming back. She knew she wouldn't sleep until she went downstairs again and checked it. The battle between sleep and knowledge lasted a good five minutes. Knowledge won.

Molly sat at the desk in the corner of the living room and punched 'play.'

"Um, hi. This is for Molly." The out-going message on the machine had been Sonia's voice. "Molly, this is Owen Palmer. I've been meaning to call you to thank you for the flower you left for me in Madison. Sorry I missed you. I met your daughter down there. Anyway, I was wondering if we could have coffee some time. I'm back in Long Lake now." He left his phone number and said goodbye.

Molly played the message back a second time, now without the surprise. She was tuning in to Owen's voice, remembering it. Her date that night and her behavior were suddenly embarrassing to her, but she wasn't sure why. It was too much for her to think about at the moment. She felt as if she only had enough energy to climb the stairs and get back to bed, but now the ascent was weightless and the pillow was cool and damp like a soft stone in the river of forgetfulness.

CHAPTER EIGHTEEN

Roland left me and the girls quite a bit of money. More money than I ever thought I'd see in my lifetime. Thank goodness he also left me with a little perspective concerning this gift. I found a passage in his third book concerning wealth and mental health, which seems to work for me. He wrote: Most people will deny to their graves the truth that money is their true god. If they put half the energy into a spiritual relation that they do into their financial arrangements, there might be more peace in this world. You see, wealth is finite; there is only so much of it on earth, but the war that rages for accumulation is never-ending. Whenever you can, hand back the gold of the earth to the powers of Heaven. Your receipt will be sleep.

It was long past bar time across the counties bordering Lake Winnebago. Most of the citizens were lying in their beds digesting perch in their stomachs and processing Old Fashioneds in their livers. There was no moon in the early hours of that Saturday and, though not a soul noticed, the wind turbines all went still when the last of the night breeze died away after 3 AM. All that could be seen of the beasts were the flashing red lights on top, which were somehow synchronized into a one dash code.

At the Holiday Inn, Karin and Leah had retired early in anticipation of the big day ahead; but as usual lately, Karin was awake and trying to remember every detail of her past life in this town. She felt like she needed the preparation. Confronting her sister should be an easy, if awkward thing to do, she thought. She wondered if she didn't over-dramatize it in her mind. It was like trying to remember a soap opera, years after it had gone off the air. Would any of the characters care if they were resurrected? Would anyone be interested in a reunion show? In the next bed, Leah was doing the rhythmic breathing of an unburdened soul. Karin was envious and longed to get to that space herself, but she knew it wouldn't come until the mission of this trip was completed.

At Pat and Bim's house, everyone was asleep except Melanie. She and Sonia were sleeping at angles to each other on a big sectional couch in the basement. She was awake and listening for squeaks in the floor above her that would signal that maybe Ray had come back down to the kitchen. If he did then she was ready to go up there and maybe talk until dawn. It had been a couple hours now and the only sound was Sonia's gentle snoring. Melanie could see her sister by the soft light of a beer sign illuminated behind Bim's basement bar. It was a diorama of a lake in a pine forest with the shore moving by as if seen from a boat. The scene kept repeating itself for the amusement of Hamm's beer drinkers. The monotony of the sign and the lack of overhead squeaks eventually put Melanie to sleep.

Up on The Ledge, Meg Bollander had fallen asleep in her chair as usual. She had been especially tired that evening after doing the long overdue housecleaning. She figured she was about half done. The work and the Kessler's had dropped her into a deep sleep, but something awakened her with a start at 3:15. She opened her eyes and listened. There were lots of critters that came by her house at night, making strange noises, but this was different. It was the sound of something she recognized, but couldn't quite place. It was a low and distant throbbing hum. Maybe a plane, she thought, circling overhead. She closed her eyes and tried to slip back into oblivion, but the sound came again, only slightly louder. Her eyes flew open as her mind identified the noise, but then she quickly dismissed the thought. How could she be hearing a wind turbine turning when the only one close enough to hear was yanked out over five years ago? She pulled her comforter up over her head and quickly dropped off once more.

Later, Molly rolled over in her bed and in a brief moment of consciousness realized she was still fully dressed from the night before. She groaned because she knew what that meant and then, right on cue, she was slightly nauseous. The previous evening came back in a wavy flash. "Never again," she whispered to herself as she rolled over on her other side. Now she was facing the window. She glanced at the window and blinked. Something was wrong. There was no light coming in from the yard light and she figured the fuse had blown again. She glanced at the radium dial of the bedside clock and deduced that dawn could not be far away anyhow. "Go to sleep, you idiot," she hissed to herself as she pounded her pillow and buried her face into it. An instant later she thought she heard a soft voice reply to her. She froze.

"Who you calling an idiot, girl?"

Molly sat up straight in her bed with her heart pounding, her eyes desperately trying to see in the dark. She thought she must have imagined the voice. Or God forbid, she was dreaming about the farmer kids under the bed again. She thought she had talked herself out of that delusion some time ago. She was just about to lay her head back down when she saw something across the room where a large over-stuffed chair sat next to her dresser. There was just a very slight luminescence emitting from that area: a silvery line that was pulsating ever so daintily, etching the blackness like a magic wand.

"You gonna answer me?"

This time Molly not only knew that the voice was real, but she knew the person who was speaking to her. She knew and yet she could not believe it. Whether it was a dream or another invitation to madness, she had to respond. "Roland?"

The light over by the chair flickered, now lightly defining a silhouette. *"Hello, Molly."*

The voice somehow did not frighten Molly. How could it? She had been hearing it in her head for five years. The voice was part of the house, part of her life and creativity. She knew she was reaching across some vast expanse that lay undefined between her bed and the chair. The moment felt sublime.

"How?" she whispered.

"Oh heck, Molly, I don't know how this works. It just does."

"Why?" Getting one word at a time out was all she could manage. They seemed to stick in her throat, lodged against her heart.

"Well, girl, I guess the simple answer is I am here because you need me."

"Yes."

"Okay, let me make this easy for you. You lay back down there and just listen to me. I don't think we have too much time. The wind is going to die down again and those things will shut down and…well, it's complicated, okay?"

Molly simply nodded at the silhouette and lay back on the pillow, but she kept her eyes open watching the source. She noticed the silver light was now blue like a gas flame.

"Messages are passed between loved ones. Those messages fill the cosmos and are driven to their destinations by longing and received by love. When I say love, I mean light within the darkness, warmth within the coldness of forever. It is an unbreakable bond, Molly. Always remember that. The feelings of love that you enjoy here are just an appetizer of the full meal that lies ahead. As humans we glimpse this notion, but lose it in the noise of the world. I came here tonight to tell you about love in the darkness and silence of night because I cannot compete with that noise."

Molly smiled and yawned spontaneously. She felt weightless and warm; a girl in the arms of her father.

"I need to tell you a quick story. It might not make sense right now, but it will. Your love story began in the ice. Long ago the ice came down here from the north. The Swift Sure Hand was finished with His painting of the sky and began to mold the land. He had an idea in His mind to make a special place that his children would enjoy: a place where they could find Him in every rock and tree. That place is where you lay right this minute, Molly. The ice came down and gouged out the lake basins, pushed up the hills, and rearranged the rocks

into a pattern as perfect as the human eye. In the iris of that eye is an imperfection that is perfect."

Molly heard the words and wanted to remember them. Roland read her mind.

"You were thinking about that damned tape recorder, eh?"

She heard him chuckle and it thrilled her.

"You don't need it. Don't worry, you'll remember everything. You don't have a conversation like this very often, do you?"

Again the familiar chuckle.

"So, okay, time is getting short. I will get to the point. Molly, my dearest daughter, you are not going mad even though you are speaking to…a ghost. The truth is neither dead nor alive. The thing that is missing in your life, the thing that you seek is waiting for you. It is perhaps hidden too well in your mothering, your sexuality, your hesitant creativity, and your swan dives into oblivion. More specifically, the girls are going to be fine women. The writing will come back when you stop blowing out its candle. Dating satyrs and drinking too much are fun until the next day dawns when you realize you are now ten steps behind your happiness. Molly, look at me."

She raised her head up and gazed hard at the light which was now soft and as yellow as dawn.

"You need to discover something that is hidden. Something that was left behind just for you. He left it for everyone, but some don't look hard enough. Molly, find the kame."

"The what?" She startled herself with the volume she had summoned. Her eyes were boring into the darkness and light that defined Roland was fading…almost gone.

"The kame," he said. And then he was gone. The departure was sudden and complete. The yard light came back on and the room became lit just enough to reveal the empty chair. Molly wanted to leap out of bed and search for him, but she couldn't move. She couldn't move because she was asleep, two layers deep into a dream within a dream.

Molly woke up to the sound of her cell phone. It was somewhere in the bed and it took a moment to locate it in the pocket of her jeans. It was Melanie.

"Hello, honey," she croaked into the phone.

"Mom? You sound hoarse," said Mel.

"Just a little. What's up?"

"Pat said I should call and tell you we are going out for breakfast and then she's bringing us home."

Molly cleared her head and recognized that Pat was giving her a warning just in case she still had company. "Tell Pat anytime is okay."

"Okay...so how was your date?"

Molly felt the first edgy wave of her hangover splashing on the shore of her brain. "Um, it was okay. We had fun."

"Do you like him, Mom? Are you going to go out again?"

"I don't know." Molly then remembered something that would get her off this awkward subject. "I heard you met someone nice last night, Mel."

"Well, yeah..." The words were drawn out in a peculiar way.

"That nice, huh?"

"Uh huh."

"Can't talk, right?"

"Uh uh."

"He's right there?"

"Uh huh."

"Talk to you later, babe. Bye."

"Bye, Mom."

Molly closed her phone and sat on the edge of the bed. Well, she thought, at least I'm already dressed. She got up and headed for the bathroom, where she washed her face and stuck a toothbrush into her mouth. She gagged on it and threw up into the sink. That act seemed to make her feel a little better. She went downstairs and stood in front of the coffee pot. The thought of coffee made the gag reflex return. She decided a walk was what she needed and grabbed a sweatshirt and headed out the door.

The world outside the house was welcoming and healing. The skies were mostly clear, but with some of those rippled clouds hanging like shingles in the southeast. Molly couldn't help but notice that the lilacs had burst into bloom over night. She smelled them first and then her eyes flew to the large bushes that marked the burial sites of both Roland and his dog, Sorry. She stared at the spot. She did remember almost every word and detail of the visitation that had occurred a few hours earlier. She tried to write it all off as a vivid dream, but she knew that whether dream or reality, it didn't matter. Papa had come home and he had spoken to her. The only thing she couldn't quite recall was his last word. Maybe it would come to her later.

As she made her way around the property, she began to feel much better. The beautiful morning would not tolerate a hangover. As she passed the site of the old turbine, she was amazed at the huge pile of branches that Sonia and Hector had collected. It was going to be quite a bonfire. That thought led her eyes up and eastward to Meg Bollander's place. If everything went according to plan tonight, Meg was going to see a ghost of her own. Molly then imitated Roland's deep chuckle and continued the healing circuit of her walk.

CHAPTER NINETEEN

I grew up in Boston, Catholic as hell, and knew just slightly more about the Red Sox than the Trinity. Some people who know me ask if I ever get homesick for New England. Well, yeah, of course I do, but if you drive over to Sheboygan and look at Lake Michigan on certain days, it's hard not to think it could be the Atlantic Ocean. I have seen days when that body of fresh water gets just as bitchy as the Atlantic, minus the clams and scrod, of course. I also retain a bit of a Boston accent, but it is slowly being taken over by Wisconsinese. I heard it first when attending Mass in Fond du Lac when the priest gave his blessing: 'Da Lort be wit chou'. The congregation replying in unison:' And also wit youse!' And I talk funny?

Sonia Costello had been the first one out of the bathroom at Pat's house that morning. She knew that Melanie, who was next in line, was going to take her time, partly because she always did, but mostly because she would be fixing herself up for Ray. Since the sleepover had been spontaneous, neither of the girls had clean clothes and Sonia knew her sister would be very conscious of that. Actually, her own first impression of Pat's grandson was very good. He was cute, but also had kind eyes and soft manners. Sonia figured he would be okay for Mel, but the distance thing was going to be a problem, which would probably kill the crushes quickly. Sonia was a deep thinker. She wandered out the back door and immediately confronted another deep thinking person.

Bim was already in the garage and icing down the day's libations. When he saw Sonia come out of the house, he whistled her over. Sonia was leery of Bim, but could not think of an excuse or an escape. She ambled slowly over to the open garage.

"Good morning there, Sunshine," Bim quipped. "Have a seat. They ain't gonna be ready to leave for a good while."

Sony shrugged her shoulders and sat in the offered lawn chair, but only after scooting it farther away from Bim's perch. She surveyed the scenery and then focused on him.

"You shouldn't drink in the morning," she said.

"Oh, is that right? What time of day is a good time to drink, you reckon, little girl?"

"Maybe no time."

Bim cracked a beer open in defiance and took a gulp, keeping his eyes on Sonia. He then burped. "Actually, you are way too young to appreciate this, but morning is the best time to drink. Look around you here. It's Saturday, springtime in Wisconsin. The birds are up and singing and the flowers are opening up all over town."

"So why do you need to drink beer to enjoy that stuff?"

"Hah, you're a sassy one, girl. And too young to understand certain complexities of life."

"Whatever." Sonia crossed her arms and stared straight ahead.

Bim thought he had better change the subject. "Looked to me like your sister and ol' Ray Jr. hit it off pretty good last night. I had to break them up in the kitchen after midnight."

The tactic worked. Sony's head snapped toward Bim. "Break them up? What happened?"

"Well, it looked like a hug, but who knows where it might have gone if I didn't come down. You young people don't waste no time, do you?"

Before Sonia could carefully consider her reply she charged to her sister's defense. "Hey, a hug is what us young people do. Besides, who are you to talk, Mr. Stouffer? My mom says your wife wasn't cold in her grave before you went after Pat." She knew in an instant that she had just indicted her mom and herself, but when she looked at Bim, he was smiling. Then he was laughing.

"Like I said, girlie, you don't know nothin'. My wife was cold long before she passed. Cold as ice, that woman was, rest her soul. And your mom is dead right in her assessment. I went after Pat like my life depended on it, because it did."

"Why did your life depend on it?"

Bim took another long sip of beer. He spotted Pat through the kitchen window working at the sink. He pointed her out to Sonia. "See that woman in there? I loved her for a long time before I asked her to marry me. She was always as warm to me as my wife was cold. We knew each other as neighbors for years, but there were never any stolen hugs at midnight in the kitchen. When my wife died Pat saved my life because I would have died without her love. A man needs to be loved and not told all the time what a shithead he is...even if he is." Bim stared at Pat in the window and shook his head. " Look at the way that light over the sink makes her look like she's got a halo. I live with an angel, little girl." His voice cracked.

Sonia saw a tear roll down Bim's cheek, but she had to ask one more question. "If you feel like that then why do you sit in the garage all day and drink beer?"

Bim sniffled, set his beer, down and looked at Sonia. "I sit out here because I find some peace in this garage. I can look at my wife in that kitchen window, where she is framed like a holy picture and thank God for her. I sit out here so she knows where to find me. You understand any of that?"

Sonia's eyes were big. She had not expected this from him. "I kind of get it, I think. I have this boyfriend named Hector and I like to look at him, too."

If you look hard enough for a common ground, there is always time for a second glance at a poorly judged book cover. And generation gaps can close in the blink of an eye. Stuff like that happens in garages.

Dr. Owen Palmer was out for a morning walk on this spectacular Saturday morning. He had decided that a hike to the top of Dundee Mountain would get his blood going and stretch out his unexercised hospital legs. Of course, Dundee Mountain wasn't exactly Mt. Everest, but it was a nice bump in the Kettle Moraine, with a view all the way to Lake Michigan on a clear day. He was about half way up the trail when his cell phone rang. He got no clue from the caller ID, but answered anyway.

"Hello, this is Owen."

There was a short pause and then a woman's voice. "How about coffee on Monday?"

"What?"

"Coffee. Monday. How 'bout it, Doctor?"

The realization that it was Molly caught him totally off guard. His location made the voice seemed somehow alien. "Molly? Costello?"

He heard her giggle. "Yes, it's Molly Costello. You call me and then you're surprised when I call you back?"

"Forgive me, okay. I'm on Dundee Mountain and the altitude is messing me up."

More giggles. "How are you feeling? Getting better, I hope."

"Well, my face looks like shit and my skin grafts are weeping. You still wanna have coffee?" It just came out.

"Yeah, I do."

Somehow it wasn't officially spring until he heard those three words.

"How about the Bagelmeister on Main in Fondy at 8 AM Monday? That work for you?" Molly continued.

"I'll be there."

"Good. See you then."

"See you then."

"Bye."

"Bye."

Local folklore has it that the top of Dundee Mountain is a landing pad for extraterrestrials. It was that morning.

On her end of the concluded phone call, Molly was feeling very happy. The day was truly going to be memorable in many ways. Although the Monday coffee date seemed a long way off, she had already made that the center piece of her week to come. But before that, there would be the epic reunion of the Bollander sisters...she hoped. Her hangover had dissipated along with her strange dream. The day was just too splendid to be dominated by the events of the night before, real or imagined. It was time to start preparing for company at Ghost Farm.

Pat had arranged for Karin and Leah to join her, the Costello girls, and her grandson, Ray at the Meadows Restaurant for breakfast. Bim declined the invitation to join the group, as was fully expected. The older ladies were having fun chatting about the various possible outcomes for the evening at Ghost Farm. Pat and Leah were optimistic; Karin was still very leery. Melanie and Ray were huddled together speaking too softly for Sonia to hear much of their conversation, but she was sure trying hard to do so. Just as Pat and Karin were fighting over the check a cell phone chirped. The sounded caused all of them to reflexively reach for their own phones. The winner was Ray.

The call made him smile at first and then his face turned dark and he stood up and walked just out of ear shot from the table to a quiet corner near the restrooms. Pat glanced at him with mild concern, but Melanie's eyes were locked on Ray and more than interested, she was scared. She was picking up his body language and it was speaking very bad news. Ray was back at the table a minute later looking composed, but not at all happy. Everyone at the table sat silently.

"That was Marcia, Crazy Ray…I mean my dad's girlfriend. Dad had a stroke early this morning and is in the hospital."

"Oh God," said Pat. "Is he going to be alright?"

"She said real bad, Grandma. Nobody knows much just yet." He was talking to Pat, but looking at Melanie. She instantly knew what all this meant. "I need to get back there," he continued.

"Of course you do," said Pat and started to wave, trying to get the waitress' attention. Karin and Leah could only observe this family scene in silence. Sonia wanted to say something, but couldn't find the words that usually just popped out of her.

Ray spoke directly to Melanie. "You and I need to talk. Right now. Outside." She got up and went to the door with Ray right behind. Everyone else just stared.

Outside in the parking lot, Ray walked to an open parking place and gently took Melanie's arm. He turned her to face him. "You know I have to go."

"I know."

"I know I just said I was going to stay for another week and then the phone rang."

"Yeah, I guess it was not meant to be." The words sounded canned.

"I'm sorry, Melanie, I wanted to get to know you this week."

She moved a step closer and put her head on his chest. His arms completed the embrace. "It's about your dad now, not us. Things like this happen in life. You don't have to worry about me."

"I'm worried about everything right now."

"I know." She wanted to cry, but couldn't. Something brave inside her had kicked in. "We just met last night, any-way. We've got cell phones and email. Maybe we'll get to know each other that way, huh? Maybe it was going too fast."

Ray looked down and Mel looked up. He smiled sponta-neously. "How come you're more mature than I am?"

"It must be my old Asian soul coming out." Her returned smiled eclipsed the sun. "I'll be eighteen next time I see you."

"When's your birthday?"

"Coming up."

Somehow Ray knew he wasn't supposed to ask exactly when. "Okay. Listen, we're okay, right?"

She nodded.

"I have to get to the airport as soon as possible so…"

"Let's just say goodbye right here, okay?" Mel now had a grip on his jacket lapels. She had a thought flicker in her head that this was just like a movie.

As the rest of their breakfast party looked out the window at them, Melanie and Ray shared their first kiss in the parking lot. Someone driving by tooted his horn playfully. Sonia knew she was watching her sister's very first kiss from a boy ever and noted that it was a pretty good one.

CHAPTER TWENTY

I have been told that in Asia Minor, in the years just after the life of Jesus, the image of the Virgin Mary was modeled after the face and figure of Athena, the Greek goddess of Wisdom. When pagan temples became churches, that Olympian symbol became an icon of Christianity. I have never had a problem with that. It seems very logical looking back that men of that age could not invent a new face the way that we invent new looks and labels for say...beer. Branding is the very soul of advertising in the 21st century. Why not in the first? Driving around the countryside of our very Catholic Holyland one sees Mary sitting in yards, perched on porches, and even resting on the dashboards of minivans. No one probably knows or cares that her face and clothing are those of a Greek goddess. She is both beautiful and serene: two things essential to the ideal of motherhood. She is timeless.

There was a certain energy of expectation in the air that exploded when a match was set to the bonfire on the former site of Roland's wind turbine. He had cut through many ribbons of red tape and spent quite a lot on legal wheel grease to have it removed from his property. His motive had been a gesture of reconciliation toward his neighbor, Meg Bollander, but that gesture had been futile. Meg had stayed true to her feelings for the man, even after his death. The pact that she made with her own stubbornness had driven her further into her own form of madness on The Ledge. Tonight it would come to its inevitable test. Little sister was back in town and she was burning up the past.

Without any real planning, the evening's festivities were beginning to take shape and the shape was a semicircle around the fire. The weather was starry and cool. Molly and the girls had carried lawn chairs, including one extra, out to the site, along with a cooler full of good wine and soda for the girls. Sonia and Melanie were given chances to opt out of the evening, but they were very curious about what was going to happen. Melanie was mostly silent since Ray's plane had already taken him away from her, but she sat with her cell phone in her hand waiting for the chime of a text or the ring of a call. He had called her from the airport in Milwaukee, but nothing in hours. She knew it was stupid to wait, but despite her maturity and intellect, she was exploring her first real crush. Everyone in the circle knew it and respected it.

Sonia had turned down a movie date with Hector to be included in the ceremony. Ceremony was her word, her concept of what was going on. She liked the ladies from California and listened to them closely. Their accents and takes on things were different and she liked that. She and Leah had bonded a bit, probably because they were kind of bit actors in the big play. Sonia sat next to Leah and they talked about the West Coast as the fire rose into the night sky.

"So now we wait, huh?" said Karin.

"Yes, we wait. Look for the headlights of an ATV coming down the hill. That'll be Meg," said Molly.

"And you're sure she'll come down?"

"Okay, listen, Karin. She sits up there day and night looking out her front window. She's up there right now and seeing this fire where there should be darkness. If she can resist coming down to investigate then I have her figured out all wrong."

Karin nodded, the fire lighting up the dubious look on her face. She took a sip of wine from a paper cup and closed her eyes. She saw Jim Salazar, the love of her life. She missed him terribly and suddenly wished that he were still alive so she would not be sitting there. When she opened her eyes, she stared into the flames and saw Roland. Not the book cover Roland, but the young and angry man, whose actions had altered her life's course. She thought that maybe tonight she could lift him out of the fire and send him off with the sparks into the night sky; the Heaven in her heart where Jim already lived. She smiled at the thought. Leah saw it.

"What are you smiling at, sis?"

"Hah," said Karin, "I was just imagining Jim and Roland looking down and seeing this display of pagan voodooism. They would probably roll over laughing."

"Roland would like this," said Molly.

"So would Jim," Leah added.

"What about voodoo?" asked Sonia.

"Oh honey, I just meant a bunch of women sitting around a bonfire is sort of occult," Karin explained to Sony, who was two chairs to her right. She had to lean out to speak to her.

"Oh, like witches?" Sony observed.

Molly laughed and had to spit out a mouthful of wine. "That's us! The Witches of Wisconsin!"

Everyone of them had a good laugh. The wine was kicking in and the fire was getting hotter. Everyone had to move her chair back a few feet from the heat.

Up above them, in a darkened living room, witch number six was glaring down at the fire. Meg had seen the blaze almost from the first spark. Her first impression was that the Costello girls were having a little Saturday night beer party. But then she realized that the fire was too big for something like that. It would draw too much attention. Also, from her perspective, it was impossible to tell if the fire was on their side of the property line or hers. That was the trigger. If the fire was on her property she was going to call the police and the fire department and raise holy hell. She quickly put on a jacket and headed out to her barn to fire up the red ATV. She planned a quick drive by and then she would come back to make her calls.

Meg drove a little slower in the dark than she normally would. She angled over to the low stone wall on the north side of her property and then headed down hill. As she got closer, she could see figures seated around the fire and was pretty sure it was some sort of a party. But, it still was a close call as to which side of the line the fire was on. She felt a wave of righteous anger break across her as her eyes narrowed like a raptor swooping in for a kill. It was the most excitement she had had on a Saturday night in years.

Leah saw the headlight first. "Looks like we have a visitor."

Everyone's head snapped towards the darkness to the east. Sure enough, there was a light bouncing downhill.

"Oh my God, that's her!" Molly gasped. She couldn't quite believe her plan was working.

"Oh shit," Karin murmured.

The girls looked at each other with raised eyebrows. This was going to be good.

Meg stopped the ATV and switched off the engine. She could not make out the faces in the flickering light, but she was pretty sure one of them was her neighbor.

"That you over there, Molly Costello?" She had to shout a little over the crackling and popping of the burning wood.

"Greetings, Meg. Com'on over and have a glass of wine with us."

Meg squinted. "Who's us?"

"Me, and the girls," Molly shouted.

"Looks like you had a couple more since the last time I saw you."

"I have company from out of town."

"And you entertain them by setting fire to half of the county?"

"That's right, Meg. And since you're here, you might as well join us for a minute. It's been a long time, neighbor."

Meg's first instinct was to ignore Molly's invitation and ride back up the hill. She had noticed now that the fire was on the site of the old turbine and just off her property and on Molly's. She was about to act on that instinct when one of the strangers called out to her.

"Margret Mary Bollander!"

Meg's head cocked to the sound of the voice. It was somehow familiar in tone and content.

"Who's that?" she called back. Nobody called her by that name. Nobody in years, anyway.

"Why don't you com'ere once and see," answered the voice.

Without thinking it over, Meg got off the four-wheeler and walked around the fire. Molly was now standing and holding out a paper cup of wine. Meg took the cup without looking or acknowledging her neighbor. She was concentrating on adjusting her eyes to find out who was being so familiar with her.

"Hello, Sis," Karin whispered.

Everyone waited breathlessly for Meg's reaction. The long lapse in the two Bollander girls' sisterhood was about to close. No one knew what to expect, but anger was not being ruled out. Meg was unpredictable, at best.

Meg looked at Karin in the firelight and did a quick, short nod. She saw the empty lawn chair next to her sister and slowly sat down. From that seat Meg first stared into the fire and then took a long gulp of wine, and then another. In the dark no one could see the tension in Meg's face melt away, but it did like a prune returning to a plum. Her dry mouth finally wetted, she spoke very softly.

"So how is California, Karin?"

"It's still there, I suppose," Karin replied.

"Ain't fallen in the ocean yet, hey?"

"Not yet."

The other spectators felt as if they were watching a scene from a play. It was fascinating, especially to the young girls.

"So, you've come home, have you?"

"For a visit, yes."

"And how long will you be here then?"

Karin decided to get to the arc of the evening. She had come so far for this moment.

"I'm staying until I get my sister back," she whispered.

Meg was still staring at the fire, but she nodded. "Might take a couple of two, three days."

"That will be fine."

Meg finally looked at Karin. There could be no real eye contact in the unsteady light. She looked around at the others. "You girls are getting big."

"Hi, Mrs. Bollander," said Melanie.

Sonia chimed in with a hi of her own.

"I can see you now, too, Molly. You're well, I take it?"

"I'm just fine, Meg."

"That leaves only one stranger," said Meg looking at Leah.

"This is my sister-in-law, Leah," Karin said.

"Sister-in-law, eh?" Meg was trying to connect those words to what little recent history she had of her sister's life. "I guess that makes us some sort of relation, eh girl?"

Leah smiled. "Let's just say we're sisters by marriage. Hello, Meg."

Meg nodded. "Well, Molly, it looks like I need a refill."

Molly stood and grabbed a wine bottle and filled her cup.

Meg thanked her with a nod. Then she began to cry. "Oh shit, I ain't wept in years and now twice in a week. Forgive me."

Like tiny leaks in a dike, water began to seep from everyone's eyes. It was as if a wicked spell had indeed been broken by this roaring bonfire. Karin reached over and took her sister's hand. Meg squeezed it right back at her. Molly felt a tidal wave of relief wash over her. The night could have gone many ways including no way. She thought about how bitterness and anger are sometimes just looking for an excuse to end. Darkness seeks out the light. It doesn't happen all the time, but a stony heart can soften if it really, really wants to. Meg had not fought it off. Maybe she had been ready for this night.

Eventually, slow small talk turned into chatter with the help of the wine. The girls lost interest and wandered back to the house, with Molly following them a short time later. Near midnight the fire was down to mostly red and gold coals and it was time for the party break up. There was still a lot of ground to cover between the sisters, but it had been a wonderful start.

"I want you two to come up to the house for breakfast. Uh, make that lunch. I have some more cleaning to do," said Meg.

"We'll come around noon then?"

"That would be fine then." Meg stood and stretched. "Well, I suppose…"

Karin stood and both of them thought about hugging, but Meg merely smiled and went over to her ride. "See you tomorrow, Karin. Goodnight, Leah." The engine started and she became a red tail light going up hill.

"I'd say that went rather well," said Leah.

"Yes it did, but she and I have some tricky ends to tie off. Tonight's magic could disappear in the light of day."

"Well, I suppose…" Leah spoke in perfect local dialect.

"Oh, shut up, you goof."

The two women hooked arms and headed back to first the farmhouse and then their hotel. Behind them the last calories of winter wood were burning off. In the eerie light of the abandoned fire, no one saw the slightly illuminated shadows of a tall man and a very large woman hovering near by, heads together in a gesture of contentment. Night birds swooped in to find flying insects that had been attracted by the dying light. Those birds were now everywhere.

CHAPTER TWENTY-ONE

I have a neighbor, Liz, who is a member of my book club so about every six weeks or so we meet at her house. She has horses. I had never spent too much time around horses, so the first time I was introduced to the herd (she has three) I was stunned, first by their size and second by their intelligence. The deliberate way they assessed me, mostly by scent, but also by sight was like being read by a life form from another planet. One horse in particular took an interest in me. He was a black gelding who cut me from the herd of readers and decided I was his. His name was Indian Summer, which I thought was neat and he spooked me at first with his insistence. A few visits later, it was I who courted him in turn. We spent some time just leaning on each other; daydreaming of a place of specie equality. Now I know that I can love a horse and a man…and it isn't too different.

Melanie slept with her cell phone under her pillow, but it never woke her up as she wanted it to. When she finally got up on Sunday morning, the first thing she noticed was that her hair smelled like wood smoke and she wanted to get into the shower quickly. Sonia beat her to it so she went downstairs to try to get upshots from last night from her mom.

"Coffee, Honey?" asked Molly when she saw the frown and crusty eyes of a restless night on her daughter's face.

"Please." Melanie broke a blueberry muffin in two parts and began to pick at it. "So what all happened up there after we left?"

"Well," said Molly as she handed Mel a mug. "It looks like the Bollander sisters are going to be okay now." Then she had a second thought. "At least it looked that way last night."

"What was it all about anyway, Mom? I never did understand all of that stuff about Papa and Meg."

"It's complicated, but Papa is gone and now the sisters are reunited."

"Oh, I get it, they fought over him."

"Well, not exactly, but there was a little love triangle going on way back when." Molly thought she needed to change the topic. "Did you hear any more from Ray?"

Melanie gave her a look that said it all.

"Well, he's got a lot on his mind with his dad. He'll check in later."

"Mmm, maybe."

Molly sat down at the kitchen table opposite Mel. "Look, Babe, the attraction you have for him happened pretty fast. I know he likes you, too, but my God, Mel, you only just met. Don't spend the day moping over the phone. If everything you are feeling is real, it will become real in time. Get it?"

"I'm just afraid I'll get mad before I get sad."

"Don't do either."

Just then Sonia came stomping into the kitchen barefoot, swathed in a too-large bathrobe with a towel on her head. She headed right for the fridge, grabbed the orange juice and plunked down at the table. Molly slid a glass over to her and Melanie watched as she took the other half of her muffin and began it pick at it.

"So how is the Queen of Sheba, this morning?" Molly asked with a bemused grin.

"The Queen is fine, Mom," Sony answered and finally flashed her trademark smile. She turned to her sister. "He call yet?"

Melanie shrugged and shook her head.

"Don't worry he will."

"Well, since you know everything, I can breathe a sigh of relief." Melanie bristled at what she heard as a patronizing comment.

"Okay, sisters, don't start." Molly then saw her opening. "By the way, you will both be glad to know I have a coffee date with Dr. Palmer tomorrow."

Eyebrows went up.

"How'd that happen?" asked Mel.

"He called me…and then I called him back. It was easy."

"Kewl," Sonia drawled. "What about the other guy from Friday night?"

"Yeah, Mom, you never told us about your date," joined Mel.

Molly played with a spoon. "Well, about that…I guess I had a good time, but well it sort of ended poorly."

"How?" asked Melanie.

"Oh heck, I don't know. It just did."

"That's no answer," Mel pressed on.

Molly looked down at her spoon toy and set it aside. Her eyes came up off the table cloth and looked at both her daughters. "Okay, the truth. I drank too much on Friday night and me and this guy sort of made out."

"Mom!" It was Sonia.

"Listen, to me, okay. Long story short, nothing happened. He left early. And then Dr. Palmer called and I sort of wished nothing had happened at all that night."

"So you like Dr. Palmer and don't like the other guy?" Sonia again.

"In a nutshell…yeah. End of story. When you two squirrels are done picking at those muffins, let's get ready to go shopping. Mall opens at 11."

Since the girls didn't say another word, Molly figured she had dodged the bullet from Friday night. She really wanted to call Karin, but figured it was too early. It was going to be a fun day Sunday in Fondy.

"This feels weird," said Karin as she and Leah pulled up to Meg's farmhouse. The property looked like it had received very little attention over the years. The flower beds were full of choking weeds, fallen tree branches lay everywhere, and the paint on the house was peeling badly. The only thing that was still pristine was the view.

"Wow, that's an amazing view of the lake from up here," said Leah. "And you grew up in this house, right?"

"I lived here until I got married to Roland. Mom and Dad used to keep it looking neat as a pin, but I guess Meg has let things go."

Just then Meg appeared in the door and the women got out of the car and walked up to the house.

"You came, eh? Thought I might have dreamed last night. Com'on in. I guess the place is as clean as it's gonna get."

Walking into the kitchen of her past life was one of the strangest moments in Karin's life. Everything looked the same, only older and shabbier. Every appliance, cabinet, table, and chair was the same only much aged by time and usage. Leah felt like she was walking through a museum diorama. It really had that feel. As they passed into the living room Meg allowed them to walk around and check out the collectibles. She had done some major dusting, but she knew she wasn't fooling anyone. There was not only an aura of another era, but there was a smell that accompanied it. Karin thought it was cleaning solutions, but Leah recognized the smell instantly. It was paint and turpentine. In the middle of the room near the window stood an empty easel.

"Do you paint, Meg?" asked Leah as Karin smiled at a white tail deer figurine that she remembered from her childhood.

"I got this itch to paint a while back, but I ain't too good at it," Meg replied.

"Do you have finished canvases?" Leah pressed.

"Nothing I want to show anyone. You two have a seat and we can have a little chat. Anyone want a drink?"

Karin smiled, but declined with a head shake. Leah followed Karin's lead, although she would not have minded something to cut the tension.

"Hope you don't mind if I do?" rasped Meg. "My throat's a tad dry today." She disappeared into the kitchen and returned with a glass of something brown served very neat.

"There are so many memories in this house, Sis." Both Karin and Leah had settled onto the couch which was covered by a yellowing chenille bedspread. Leah immediately noticed Roland's last book on the coffee table. The bookmark was early in the pages.

"Jah, we got some memories around here and little else," said Meg after she swallowed a gulp of her drink. "Mom collected a bunch of junk and then I collected a bunch more. I did it until I ran out of shelf space. Silly isn't it all?"

"No, I think it is very nice…unique," said Leah trying keep things upbeat.

"Well, thank you for saying so," said Meg, "Even if it ain't true." She winked at Leah to let her know that her point had been taken with humor. "I see you looking at that book, Leah. You read his stuff?"

"I have read all of his stuff." Somehow the name Roland was not coming out.

"You like it then, I suppose?"

"Immensely."

"How about you, Karin?"

Meg had again cut to the chase very quickly. It seemed that Roland was going to come before lunch.

Karin took a deep breath. "Meg, I am not going to beat around the bush. I came here to speak to you about Roland and now's as good a time as any."

Meg nodded and took another gulp. Leah got up and asked where the bathroom was, although she knew it couldn't be too hard to find.

And so the Bollander sisters finally began a conversation that had been avoided for almost thirty-three years. It was mostly one-sided. Karin began by going back to the night of the fight in '81 and the punch, which she now confessed to have provoked. She told Meg about the emotional affair she had with Jim Salazar over the years and how she wanted out of her marriage. She described her escape to California and admitted that she never intended to come back or set foot in Wisconsin again. Most painfully, she confessed to Meg that she had shredded their relationship because she never thought she could look her in the eye. For what had happened between the two of them, she asked her sister to blame her and forgive Roland. The words 'forgive Roland' entered Meg's brain and caused a minor short circuiting. It was a concept she had never, ever considered for even a minute over those years. And now her sister was requesting it.

Meg set her drink down and hung her head. "I am not sure I can do what you ask."

"I'm not asking you to forgive me, Sis, but he was all messed up in those days and I used it against him for my own purposes. I wanted him to hit me and he did. I wanted to leave him and he fell into my trap to make it happen. Let it go, Meg. God knows I am trying to."

Leah was still hiding in the bathroom, but she could hear pretty much every word. As things got quiet, she decided to wander out, but maybe find some other room to hang out in until this was over. She saw a door across the hall and pushed it open. Suddenly, she had just stepped into the most astonishing room she had ever entered. It was literally filled with finished canvases and in an instant her appraising expertise told her she had walked into an artistic gold mine. Meg's oils were not only good; they were the work of a very talented eye and hand. She started to count and came up with around one hundred and ninety-five various sized visions of Lake Winnebago. Each of them a masterpiece. And the colors, the blends were amazing. She was bursting at the seams to tell Karin, but then realized that the paintings had been hidden away from them for a reason and she needed to respect that. She wouldn't mention the art until they left the house.

The living room had gone quiet. Meg got up and walked to the window and looked out at the view that was imprinted on her mind like no other. Without turning around, she spoke to her sister.

"I'm not sure any of this changes anything because we can't undo the past, Karin. I lived a whole lot of days hating Roland and those days never came off no calendar in my mind. If he was in this room right now I don't know if I could forgive him."

"I understand and I'm sorry," Karin said, trying to be soothing. She knew Meg's wounds were incurable.

Meg suddenly whirled around. "Sorry! Hah, that was the name of his damned dog! Sorry! Turned out he loved that barking mutt more than anything…anyone."

Meg then raised her chin and straightened her spine. Karin thought she looked pretty again, framed by the window and backlit sunlight. "Let me think some more about all of this. He is one thing and you are another. We are blood, so I guess you and I are going to have to make some sort of a move away from those days."

"Yes, we are."

"Come on back in here, Leah. I know you're a'listening in there. We are about to have a Bollander toast."

Leah came slowly back into the living room. Her eyes were now seeing Meg in a totally different light. She flashed on Karin, who wore an expression of surprise.

Meg went into the kitchen and came back with a dusty bottle and two more glasses. She poured about three fingers of the contents of the bottle into each glass and handed them to the other two. Both Karin and Leah smelled the contents and winced.

"What is this stuff?" asked Leah.

"It's called Vermox. It's vile, but it's a soul cleanser and that's what we need here."

"You want us to drink this?" said Leah with a grimace.

"You two didn't know it, but you came all the way across the country to drink this shit, girl."

Meg held her glass up and gestured that Karin and Leah should do the same. "We gonna do a toast and then we put all this behind us, okay. No more talk about nothing."

"Okay, Sis, whatever you say."

In the room where Meg had spent ten thousand nights cursing her world and the people who populated it, she had finally come to her sublime moment. It wasn't forgiveness and it wasn't exactly forgetting. It was only a simple toast, made humbly and honestly.

"Fuck the past!"

They all drank and gagged at the same time.

CHAPTER TWENTY-TWO

I wonder some times if men know how much we women embrace the mystic. In my lifetime I have never questioned the presence of ghosts because the church and catechism was all about them. I have always looked for omens in the sky and signs of coincidence. I don't wake up without wondering about the magic of the dawn or the mystery of the sky. Stars are not just points of light to me, but destinations of the heart. If this sounds overly romantic, it is! I refuse to live in a world that is determined by Dow Jones or based on sexual and economic conquest. My inner world is spooky and I like it that way. On certain nights I feel the ocean inside of me. I never have given birth, but I am certain that the ocean and the breaking of waves is essential to that miracle. Women are old souls and we cannot escape that role. I love being earth mother. I love being mystic. I love.

There was a dense fog on Monday morning that seemed to be especially thick as Molly drove around the bottom of Winnebago towards her date with Owen. Despite the murky weather she was in high spirits. There was an exciting feeling that something wonderful was lurking out there in the mist, waiting just for her. Of course, she had counseled herself that her expectations were too high. After all, she had met Owen and been in his company for only a fraction of time that Melanie had spent with Ray, and yet she had warned her daughter about flash attractions. She smiled to herself when she recognized the fact that she never had been able to take her own advice. She frowned when she remembered that Melanie had still not heard from Ray since Saturday.

Before she got too deep into her psyche, she arrived at the Bagelmeister. Luckily, there was a space in the two hour free parking area on the street. It was going to be an interesting two hours. The coffee shop was mostly empty, so it was not hard for her to spot Owen sitting against the wall. His back was to the door and he was reading the paper. As she approached him from behind, she remembered what Melanie had said about his face. Don't flinch, she told herself.

"Owen?"

He turned around and saw the owl lady for the first time in three months, three lifetimes, actually. He glanced quickly and remembered how pretty she was and he reflexively looked down.

"Hello, Molly, good to see you again."

She got it. She sat down and set her purse on the table. "Look at me." He did. "I am so happy to see you again. Don't look away. Let me see you."

It was a hard request for him to obey, but he did it. "Not so pretty, huh?"

The inventory included one mostly missing eyebrow, one purple puncture hole in the left cheek, three long scars down the right side of his head from the ear to his throat, and some miscellaneous scarring around the lower lip and chin. There was some obviously new dental work, too. Molly took it all in and then saw the kindness and insecurity in his eyes. "It's okay," she said. She actually liked the fact that his hair had grown long. "How is the rest of you?"

"Well, I won't be posing for *Playgirl* anytime soon."

"That's a good thing."

"I guess."

"Hey, okay, we got that over with. How do you like your coffee?"

In the next hour, Molly and Owen talked about everything under the sun…or fog. He told her about his practice drying up and she told him about her recent anxiety and writer's block. They went back and forth with ease. They went back to the day they had met and talked about the owl and how the kids handled the loss. It was a slow dance, but a sincere attempt to get to know each other. They both felt comfortable in each other's company, just as they had from the first minute. Then Molly needed to know some things about the rest of that fateful day.

"So the cat…what happened to it?"

"Well, it actually stayed alive for a while at the State Animal Lab down in Madison."

"For a while?"

"When I got out of the hospital, I went to see it."

"You're kidding?"

"No, see Molly, I sort of had to." She nodded. "It was in such bad shape that I asked to euthanize it."

"Oh my god, you mean you killed the cat that attacked you? As an act of compassion? Wow!"

"I *am* a veterinarian. And yes, I felt sorry for the cougar. She was trapped in a scenario she could not handle. We just happened to cross paths."

A moment happened. "Like us?"

Owen looked into his coffee cup for the answer to that question. Sometimes it is best if you just say something and worry about it later. Now was one of those times.

"Molly, I dreamed about you when I was in the hospital. I don't remember the details, but I know it was you. You came to me in a fever dream and I think you helped me turn away from giving up and just dying. I am not feeding you a line, okay. It was real. How do you think such things happen?"

Molly stroked the space between her eyes for a second, thinking of some way to respond. Suddenly, it was obvious. "I had a strange dream of my own just the other night. It was so real. I dreamed that my adoptive father, Roland Heinz, came to my room and told me something important, but I can't quite remember what it was. Anyway, yeah, I do believe I could have been in your head. Maybe we dream what we want to happen. See people we want to see."

"Maybe."

The word lingered in the air as Molly looked over Owen's shoulder and saw a big black pickup truck park in front of the shop. The logo and lettering on the door was unmistakable. Before Molly could hope that JB Bondurant was heading into another store, he was coming into the coffee shop with his eyes riveted on her. It's amazing, she thought, how often worst case scenario comes up in life. Freakin' Murphy's Law.

"Hey, Molly, I thought that was your Subaru parked out there. Small world, eh?"

"Sure is. Um, JB Bondurant this is Owen Palmer." They looked at each other and nodded.

"Holy shit, man! That must have been some kinda fight. I sure hope you won, but I gotta say it don't look like it. Shit!" JB never was able to hold a subtle thought.

"JB, that's an awful thing to say…"

Owen cut in. "No, it's okay. Yeah, I got into a fight and I lost badly." He had already picked up on the notion that this guy and Molly had something going. The territorial piss was already spraying around the room from this guy. Belittling the other guy was a tactic in that game and Owen knew he couldn't win the face or strength contests anymore.

Sensing weakness, JB sat down in the chair next to Molly and put his arm across the back of her chair. More territorial bullshit.

"So, Molly, did that fuse ever blow again after the other night? I could maybe come out and check it out again…you know?" JB leaned in and sniffed her like she was in heat.

Irish girls from Southy never let a situation get out of control and it was time to tap into those roots on Main Street in Fond du Lac. "JB, Owen and I were having a private conversation. I would appreciate it if you would let us finish it."

JB looked them both over and then put his palms up in a sign of submission. False submission. "Oh excuse me, but you weren't giving me no cold shoulder the other night." He winked at Owen. "Maybe when you get done with the freak show here, you can give me a call and get your fuse replaced." He stood and glared at Molly. "On second thought, you just may be a little too old for me." He turned again and smiled at Owen. "These pre-menopausal chicks can't hold their liquor." Another lewd wink.

Owen stood up and knowing his face had nothing to lose, took two steps into JB's shadow. "Get out of here, shithead!"

JB cocked his fist and did a feint punch. "I don't want to get my hand wet with that mush you call a face, pal. You two have a nice day, okay?"

That was it. JB walked out without a fight because, Molly knew, there was nothing to fight about. If she had slept with him, he would have decked Owen. The blown fuse had started dominos tumbling and she was beginning to appreciate it even more.

"Sorry, Owen, he's an ass."

"Yeah, but a big ass." Pause. "You and him…?"

"I went out with him once. I shouldn't tell you this because it breaks all the secret codes of women, but we didn't do anything that would warrant his Tarzan and Jane bullshit. Okay?"

Owen sat back down and smiled at Molly. "Okay," he said and she saw a beautiful man looking at her the way she wanted to be looked at.

Just then, the ever present and eternal cell phone chirped in Molly's purse. It was Melanie bearing sad news. Crazy Ray Hitowski, local guitar hero and rock and roll legend, had died in Los Angeles. All Molly could do was listen and say 'uh huh' over and over. Melanie was doing some secondhand grieving for a man she had never met, but because of Ray Jr. she was involved. Molly told her to hang in there until she got home, which she assured her would be soon. Owen picked it up.

"You gotta go."

"Yeah, my daughter has just entered a new world and she has no compass to navigate it."

"Interesting coffee klatch here, Molly." The smile through the scars was breaking down every wall Molly had ever put up. She looked over Owen's shoulder and saw the sun shining down on Main Street. In that instant she knew for sure what she had suspected since the day of the owl's death. This guy was the one. Everything from here on in was just going to be fine. They quickly exchanged cell phone numbers and email addresses along with promises to talk again very soon. As she stood up, though, she had a moment of lightheadedness. She remembered something in that instant that she thought she had forgotten. It was so clear, coming from a voice inside her head that was so familiar.

"Owen, what is a kame?"

He looked puzzled at first and then got it. "You mean a kame like in the Kettle Moraine? A glacial kame?"

"Uh, maybe."

"A kame is a pile of boulders left by the glaciers. Usually in a flat field."

Recognition is a blinding light and it dazzled Molly. Roland had told her to look for the kame. Now she knew what it was and Owen had something to do with it.

"Okay, listen, I am going to call you tonight," she said. "You gonna be around?"

"Yeah, I am going to be around…waiting for you to call."

On the way home Molly called Pat and got a few more details about Crazy Ray. There was going to be a memorial service in Fond du Lac next Friday. The body was coming home to be buried. Apparently, that was his wish and although his parents were dead, there still were lots of Hitowski relations and rock and roll fans still living in the area. Molly knew that meant Ray Jr. would be coming back to town and she wondered how that would affect Melanie. Of course, Mel would be glad to have him back so soon, but it might create more bonds that would have to break when he left again. Then for the first time, Molly saw a complete picture of what had happened to the women of Ghost Farm. All three of them were in love. It was a simple thing, but also very complex. She wondered if all of them were going to see their relationships grow into mature love. What were the odds? Owen, Ray, and Hector; she was pulling for all of them.

"And you counted almost two hundred paintings?" Twenty-four hours after Leah's revelation about her sister's hidden talent, Karin was still trying to comprehend the discovery. The two women were sitting in their room at the Holiday Inn trying to plan out the week. Leah needed to get back to her gallery in Santa Barbara, and Karin was mostly missing her own bed. But, it was complicated.

"Yep, and I want to show her in my gallery. I want the world to see what your sister has done."

"I am going to have to see this wonder to believe it."

"You don't trust me?"

"Well, yes, but you say they all are paintings of her view of the lake. Doesn't that sort of smack of some sort of dementia? I mean, what are we opening up here?"

Leah sighed deeply. "Look, I hate to be the one who breaks this to you, but many great artists are freaking nutcases. They are using a part of the brain that you and I can't even imagine. Meg's work is world class. Trust me on that. She could sell those canvases for a fortune."

"And you want a piece of the action?"

Leah threw her hands up in the air. "Karin baby, what do you want me to do? I own an art gallery and by some miracle...your miracle, I discover the next Monet. Or Grandma Monet! Am I supposed to just ignore what I saw?"

"I get your excitement, but what about her?"

"Am I gonna rock her world or yours?"

That question was what Karin was trying to avoid. The goal behind the trip to Wisconsin was accomplished on a basic level and now, when an exit plan was needed, Leah was unpacking monkey wrenches. In her moment of silence, Karin was trying to figure out how she was going to sneak back out of town without the twin gorillas of Roland and Meg following her. After all, she was the instigator of all his writing and he was, no doubt, the instigator of all her paintings. In essence she had diminished herself into a footnote of the literary and art world. A tiny footnote, at that. It is always hard to assume the role of some one who defers to power.

"What do you want to do, Leah?"

"You sure you want to know?"

"Talk."

"I want to take your sister and some of her art back to California."

"She might say no..."

"She probably will say no, but you asked me what I want." Pause. "And think about this while you are digesting all of this. I think your sister needs to get out of that house and see a little bit of this wider world. It looks to me like she is stuck in a

Twilight Zone of figurines and drinking. And maybe she could use another subject for her painting besides what's just outside her picture window. Karin, she showed some sense up there yesterday. She understood that the past is a boat anchor. Let's at least offer a way to change things. You know what else I think?"

"What?"

"If you disappear, she will, too. It will be like you never came home. In one week this whole trip will be erased. Think about that."

Karin was always amazed by Leah. She had some of the same qualities that her brother had: logic and love in the big picture. Karin knew that her own weaknesses had always tried to undo her. She was too pretty to think, her mother used to say. Now she thought hard.

"I want to see the paintings."

CHAPTER TWENTY THREE

The photo book that Mike Gabler did on my father just before his death was eventually titled, 'The Story of Roland,' after a Norse myth. The book was amazing and although photo essay books don't sell that well when dealing with a literary celebrity, Mike's book did well. In every review I could find in print or on the internet, the reviewers were transfixed by the cover photo, which I inadvertently had something to do with. When Mike was shooting Roland in our living room, I happened to pull into the driveway at the exact nano-second that Mike hit his shutter. A ray of sunlight reflected off my windshield, went through the window and lit up Roland's face. In the years since that coincidental miracle, I have had to think long and hard about that moment every time I see that book on my own coffee table. It always makes me think about time and chance and no matter how I turn it over in my mind it reminds me that God is one hell of a creator: even to being creative within his own creations. OMG!

Sonia had somewhat taken advantage of the situation at home, what with her mom's new excitement about Dr. Palmer and her sister's similar feelings about Ray coming back, to slip out to dinner with Hector on a school night. It would not be a night out at a restaurant she was told, but merely a simple meal at the place where the men from Mexico lived. She had never been there and was very curious because Hector never spoke about his house. She knew something was up when Hector arrived to pick her up in taxi cab.

"Why are we going in a cab?" Sonia asked as she ducked into the back seat. She noticed that the driver looked familiar.

"This is my uncle's cab. It's okay."

But Sony could tell by the look on Hector's face that things were not okay. He looked worried, maybe even scared. "What's going on, Hector? I don't like the way you're not looking at me."

Hector now looked at Sonia and forced a smile. "I will tell you at dinner, okay?"

Her instincts told her something was very wrong, but she nodded in compliance anyway.

The cab drove for about fifteen minutes to the outskirts of Fond du Lac. It turned onto a frontage road for Hwy 41 and pulled up to what was once a roadside motel now turned into cheap apartments. It was a rundown and sad place to live, she thought.

"This is where I live," Hector announced.

Sonia was silent. It did not look like a place she should be hanging out. Her mom would be appalled. Since there was no choice, she decided to trust Hector. They went into one of the little rooms. The first thing Sonia noticed was the delicious smell of food. There was a small efficiency kitchen and a big iron skillet was bubbling away. She had expected the room to be crowded with Hector's dad's brothers and friends, but there was only Hector and his father, who greeted her warmly.

"Miss Sonia, please excuse this humble place where we live."

"Hi, Mr. Marquez, that smells really good."

"I hope you like chili verde. Not so fancy, but good food."

Antonio Marquez heated tortillas in a skillet on the other burner of the two burner stove. He laid a generous portion of the pork and pepper mix into the tortillas, folded them, and put them on a platter. At the table, the men closed their eyes and then crossed themselves, giving silent thanks for the meal. As Sonia watched, she again heard a chord inside her being struck. It was the simplicity of poverty meeting the complexity of faith. She knew then that whatever Hector was going to tell her would be okay. She had faith, also. Mr. Marquez was the first to speak,

"It tastes good, Sonia?"

She nodded and said, "Yes, very good. You are a good cook."

He smiled. "Thank you, I try." Then he got to the point. "We...Hector and I have some news for you and we..." He looked at his son. "I wanted you to be here, in this place to hear it."

Sonia was confused. "What news? Why do I have to be here?" She turned to Hector, who was not eating and looking down at his plate.

"Okay, listen to me and I will explain," began Mr. Marquez. He took a deep breath and dabbed his mouth with a paper napkin. "Do you know what the INS is?"

Sonia shook her head.

"It is the immigration people. Their job is to find illegals. The man we work for was tipped off that the INS was working this area looking for illegal workers, arresting and deporting them back to Mexico. Two days ago they stopped the car with my two brothers and arrested them for not having documentation. The car was registered to me, but the tags are expired so now they are probably trying to find me, too. It is only a matter of time before they come here. Do you understand?"

"I think so." said Sony. She was already starting to put two and two together.

"Maybe a little, eh? It is a game we play when we come up north to work, Sonia," the father went on. "Like a cat and a mouse, okay? In the old days, it was not so hard, but politics have changed and so the game has changed. Do you understand what I am telling you?"

Sonia was smart and intuitive; she knew. "You are going back to Mexico?" She aimed the question at Hector.

"Yes," he whispered.

Sonia's eyes went from face to face, son to father, father to son. Her heart began to break for the first time in her life. It was like a heavy field stone had been laid on her chest. She could not stop the tears. "When?"

"We are leaving tonight, Sonia," said Hector. He wanted to hug her, but his father's eyes riveted him to his chair. Sonia saw that control being exercised.

"So why did you have to tell me here, Hector?"

Mr. Marquez answered for him. "This was my decision, senorita. You two must say *adios* right here with me in the room. You see, I fear *amor joven*."

"You fear what?"

Hector jumped in to interpret. "He fears young love. My father thinks we should not be trusted to say goodbye alone."

Sonia got the drift. She now understood what was implied and looked hard at Hector and then his father. "That wouldn't have happened."

"Maybe, maybe not. It is for the father to, how you say, buy the insurance policy," said Mr. Marquez. "I don't mean to be cruel, Sonia, but it would not be good to leave anything behind. It is possible that you will not see each other again."

Sonia was turning fourteen in three days, but she thought she already knew who she was in her world. This scenario had never even entered her head, but her mind was quick to negotiate twists and turns in the road. "I see. So this is a goodbye dinner with a chaperone?"

"Yes, Miss Sonia."

"I am sorry, Sonia," said Hector. In the depth of his heart, he had sensed this day would come all along. He had heard all the stories over the years about experiences in the north. If you find a love, you say goodbye before you say hello, he had been told.

"But, there are less than two weeks left of school. Isn't there some way…" She knew this tack was futile even before the thought was complete. Anger was beginning to mix with sadness. Hector's eyes were again focused on the table. He was shaking his head slowly.

In the end they parted without a hug or even another word. There was nothing really to say. She rode home in the back of the cab and even the uncle would not look at her in the mirror. She turned to the window and watched the scenery slide by. Unexpectedly, at this improbable moment a vision came into her head. It was a strong and vivid vision that she understood had been triggered by what had just occurred. Outside the car window, Sonia Costello was looking at Wisconsin, but she was seeing Africa. There was a valley filled with colorful, yet tattered tents. People milled about waiting for the next meal…or the next attack. Survival and warfare, the evil twins of Darfur. Sonia felt the warrior in her rise up. Fourteen years old was an old lady in Darfur; an old soul. On that evening, Hector was not the only one going home. She would go, too, and she prayed for both of them as they sped off in opposite directions.

"So when's the wedding?"

Molly knew the voice, but was having trouble placing it somewhere besides a garage. Bim had come up behind her at the grocery store and couldn't resist the jab.

"I thought you were shackled to that lawn chair, Mr. Stouffer. And what's all this about a wedding?"

"Hah, don't be coy with me, girlie. Pat never could keep no secrets. I heard about you and the veterinarian…after I heard about you and the electrician. I heard you chose bachelor number one, the animal doc. That right?"

Molly glanced around to make sure no one was listening in to this sort of personal gossip. Somehow she found herself liking to play Bim's game of attack and smile. "Why ask if you know all the answers?"

"Always like to get it from the horse's mouth."

"That's flattering."

"Oh yeah, sorry, Mol. Listen, I was pulling for the vet all along. I know the Bondurant kid by way of his family and they are the bottom of the cheese barrel around here. He fancies himself quite a rooster to the local henhouses. Glad to hear you resisted."

Molly was trying to figure out how much Pat had leaked about JB. Bim was waiting for a reply and she noticed his mouth was hanging open in anticipation of either confirming or gleaning some dirt. "Actually, Bim, I was drunk the night I went out with JB and almost did make a mistake."

"But, you didn't."

"No, I didn't."

"Just checking your story against Pat's."

"Are all you men assholes, or what?"

Bim smiled as he maneuvered his cart down the aisle. "Every last one of us, Molly." He chuckled and was gone.

Two aisles later Molly was stuck on Bim's last words. Surely Owen was not of them? But it was true she had called him and left a message three days ago, but he had not returned her call and she was damned if she was going to grovel. The idea made her angry and in the checkout aisle, when asked to choose between paper or plastic, she snapped at the bagger. "Give me whatever the hell you want!"

Melanie's luck was running better than her mom or sister. Ray was coming in tonight ahead of the memorial tomorrow. She knew she shouldn't be giddy about a funeral, but it was hard not to look at how fortune had brought this guy back so soon. She was, however, totally perplexed by Sony's behavior since two nights ago. Mel knew she had sort of snuck out to see Hector, but Sonia would not talk about what had happened. Not one word, which was unusual for her. She seemed to be glued to the computer and was printing out page after page of some sort of research she was doing. It couldn't be for school because the year was over next week. She decided to probe a little.

"So, what is all this stuff, Sony? You have a late term paper of something?"

"No."

Melanie leaned in to look at the screen of the laptop.

"And don't look of over my shoulder!" Sony snapped the lid shut on the computer.

"Okay, okay, but you are acting strange the past couple of days. I know it has something to do with Hector so if you can't tell your sister, who can you tell?"

"I don't want to talk about it."

"Okay, then will you tell me what all this data downloading is all about?"

Sonia wanted to talk more than anything. She wanted to talk about Hector's leaving, but talking would be like reliving it. She knew she would cry and act like a baby. She decided to give Melanie something. "I am researching NGO's. Do you know what that is?"

"Of course." Melanie knew everything. "Non-Government Organizations. Freelance do-gooders, right?"

"Right."

"So what's the connection?"

"I am going to join an NGO when I graduate from high school."

"You're not going to college? Mom won't let you, Sony."

"I can do whatever I want to do with my life."

"I thought you wanted to be a writer. You'll need a college education to follow that path, Sony."

"I plan to follow a couple different paths. I want to go to my first home. I want to go to Darfur and write about it. The best way to go is with an NGO."

"Wow! That's actually sort of neat. But, geez, sis, you may change your mind ten times before you get out of school. I think this has something to do with Hector. Please tell me."

Sonia heard the 'please' and in some way it allowed her to talk. "He went back to Mexico."

Melanie's mind immediately filled in the blanks; closed the gaps in the past couple of days. She sat down next to her sister and put her arm around her. "Why?"

"INS."

"Oh, no. I am so sorry. You should have told me or Mom."

"I didn't want to ruin the happiness you guys are living right now." Sonia started to cry, but caught herself. Humor was an option. "Three stupidly happy women in one house would have been insane."

"Noooo, it wouldn't."

"That's why I didn't want to talk." Sonia got up and stretched. "Don't tell Mom, okay?"

"Okay, but why?"

"Let her be happy without worrying about me for a while. She has been so weird lately that I am more worried about her than I am about my own dumb life. Promise?"

"I said I wouldn't say anything. Can't you call Hector or something?"

"No, there is no cell phone number or anything. I think his father is against us staying in touch."

"Why would he want that?"

Sonia wiped her eyes and cleared her throat. "He fears *amor joven*."

"What?" asked Melanie.

"Go look it up. It means 'bullshit' in Spanish."

Molly got home just minutes after her daughters had their tête-à-tête and she immediately picked up on it. She studied both of their faces and decided not to probe. One of them was going to bust sooner or later. She had already figured out something had happened with Hector. He had been around almost daily lately and then he was missing. That fact matched Sonia's mood swing. Molly also knew about the interest in Darfur and the NGO's. Sonia's search history was all over the computer that they all shared. Besides, she had her own problems.

But if Molly had only checked her own email she would have found her answer. Later that night when she finally did, she read a rather cold email that informed her that Owen had gone back to Madison for more plastic surgery. At first she was mad that he didn't call her, but then she thought about it. Owen's pride was wounded along with the rest of him. The encounter with JB could not have made him feel any better about his looks. Although Molly would have taken him just the way he looked on Monday, she understood his position.

Before they all went to bed, Molly called for a summit conference in her room. As they had done since their very first nights of adoption, the girls crawled in with Mom and put their heads on the pillow next to hers.

"Okay, Sonia, do you want to start?"

"No."

"Okay, listen, I know Hector and you have split up. What goes?"

"He went back to Mexico." It just came out. It had to.

"I see. I am sorry, dear. Are you going to be okay?"

"It hurts, Mom." There were no tears now, but there was pain in her voice.

Molly squeezed her. "Lots of stuff is going to hurt. Our only defense against hurt is having ourselves to lean on. When either of you hurt you need to share it."

"And you, too, right, Mom?" sniffled Sonia.

"Right. But I am guessing only one of us is hurting tonight. Mel?"

"I'm okay tonight, Mom." Then she thought it over some more. "Might be hurting in a day or two, though. I'll get back to you guys."

The way she said it caused Sonia to giggle. Molly tried to tickle Melanie, but she squirmed away, though not too far. The Costello women slept close the rest of the night. There was no ghost in the room or in any of their dreams.

CHAPTER TWENTY-FOUR

As we enter love affairs from time to time, we must still live out our lives in very mundane ways. Teeth must be brushed and toilets must be cleaned. Forgive me using those two examples in the same sentence, but it underscores my point. Love is a madness that lifts daily life above the street level of our breaths and heartbeats. It is a cosmic connection that has nothing to do with schedules or anything two-dimensional. I have thought about this a lot lately and I have come to think that love is, as the French have always known, a form of madness. Being madly in love is redundant. It is an insanity encouraged by popular music and movies. It is a dementia preyed upon by merchants of candy, flowers, and sentimental cards. But somewhere in the human psyche for the writer, there is a way out of all the madness and it is called poetry. Words of love without the music are not cures, but explanations. Unfortunately, not all of us can explain how crazy we have become.

Karin and Leah were taking Meg out to lunch. The location was Meg's choice and she chose the little pub in Johnsburg across from her church. They supposedly had a good burger basket although Meg had never tried it. Food was pretty low on her priorities of daily consumption. It was Leah's first real encounter with Holyland drinkers and she was fascinated. The ladies sat at the bar because the one and only table was unavailable. By the looks and smells of the patrons, they were mostly farmers grabbing a beer and burger between plantings, or milkings, or whatever they were up to.

"I'm charmed," Leah quipped as she surveyed the room.

"Yeah well, it'll take a couple of drinks to charm me," said Meg.

"What do you recommend, sis?" said Karin, who was not as charmed as either of them. She knew these country bars were haunted by her ex and maybe that was why Meg had coaxed them up here into the hinterlands. After just a few days, they were already reverting back into a sisterhood that had been anything but comfortable in the long gone days of country bars.

"I recommend the Dom Perignon," snarked Meg. "But they don't got none or wouldn't even know if they did."

"Funny," Karin drolled. "And where did you learn about expensive champagne?"

"I used to watch the TV, before I got other interests."

Karin and Leah exchanged California glances. It was those 'other interests' that they meant to pursue today.

The bartender finally ambled over. "Ain't seen you in a while, Mrs. Bollander. Thought we lost you to some other place."

"It's cheaper to drink at home, Karl."

"I suppose, but don't you miss your friends?"

"If I had any."

Meg had revealed too much about her lonely life already. The smart talk ended abruptly and drinks and burgers were ordered. Meg, who was sitting between the two ladies, gave them both a glance, "Okay, which one of you is going to tell me what's on your collective minds? I haven't lived this long not to know when some stray laundry is dangling on my line."

Karin took a sip of her screwdriver because she thought she was going to need its contents to get through the next few minutes, but Leah came to her rescue.

"Meg, it's me who has something to say to you. And all I ask is that you listen to me before you go off," Leah began.

Meg had an astonished look on her face. "What's all this about now?"

"Meg, when we came up the other day to your house, I wandered into your bedroom. I saw the paintings."

Meg nodded, looking a bit piqued that Leah had snooped, but she'd promised to listen so she let her continue.

"Something you don't know about me, Meg, is that I own an art gallery in Santa Barbara. I have been in the art business for almost twenty-five years and your paintings are the most spectacular oils I have ever seen. Do you have any idea how good you are?"

Meg could only grip the bar in silence. She had been busted and praised in the same minute and did not know quite how to react. "Can I talk now?" she asked.

Leah nodded.

"I think you're as crazy as a loon, girl. I made those paintings to kill the time until I die up there on The Ledge. I was snockered when I did half of them! And you say they are works of art? How can that be?"

"*That* is how art happens, Meg. Nobody sits down one day and says I am going paint a masterpiece. Certain people just do. You just did it and that's what makes it fantastic."

Meg looked at Karin who nodded in agreement with Leah. Meg emptied her Kesseler's and water. "Okay, so what if you're right? How does that change a damned thing?"

"Change only comes if you let it," Leah continued. "I want to take some of your canvases back to California with me and show them in my gallery. More than that, Karin and I want you to come back with us for the showing. Think of it as a vacation. It'll be fun."

"Why, I couldn't leave my place," said Meg.

"Honey, you're not leaving it," assured Karin, "we're only talking about a few weeks. I think it would be good for all of us.'

Meg looked stern. "This ain't no joke right?" Then another thought flashed across her mind. "This ain't no plot to get me into one of them nuthouses out there?"

Leah, almost spit out her drink. When she composed herself, she couldn't resist the plain truth. "Meg, there is not a nuthouse on earth that would take you!" Then softer and more seriously, "You have a great talent, lady. I think it is time to share it."

Meg was truly perplexed and she found a quick way out. "Well, let me sleep on it, okay girls?" she said.

Karin, who never thought the idea would get that far, smiled behind Meg's bowed head at Leah. They ordered another round and stayed at Karl & Vi's for two more hours playing pinball. It was the best time any of them had in years.

Back at University Hospital, Owen was sitting in a recovery room after his outpatient procedure to fix a couple of rents in his face. The work had been painless, but he was awake through the whole process and that alone was disturbing to him. In order to remove himself from the surgery, he had willed his mind back into his childhood. He had grown up on a farm just outside of Eau Claire, Wisconsin and his early years had been difficult. He was the only child of parents that were divorced before he was two years old. Oddly enough it was his father who raised him as his mother had disappeared. He found out by accident later that she had killed herself because she couldn't face cancer. Some unkind aunt told him she took a gun to her head because of a tumor in her breast. He had no idea what that meant until much later. His dad drank quite a bit, too, but seemed to enjoy it so his life was not as tragic. After Owen got into pre-med in Madison, his dad moved to Las Vegas, Nirvana by the Dam. They stayed in touch, but only on an infrequent level. There was no other family, except an aunt in Georgia, whom he visited from time to time. They also exchanged stupid post cards over the years.

To survive being unloved as a child, Owen did a predicable thing; he fell in love with animals. Becoming a veterinarian was a logical next step for him. He wanted to heal and protect those who healed and protected him. No one knew how deep this feeling went. No one human, at least. The last feral thought that the cougar that disfigured him had before the contents of the euthanasia syringe sent her off to oblivion was that this man who killed her also loved her. He knew that because the cat spoke to him. He could never tell anyone about that channel of communication because they would write him off as an eccentric animal doctor, a Dr. Doolittle. Or worse, a quack. In Owen's mind the universe was a noisy place and the animals of earth were godly voices spoken with eyes. Owen loved that cougar more than anything he had ever encountered and the fact that they met on the same day that he met Molly was magic. Black, dark, sun, moon magic. And yet there were problems. There always was.

Ray Hitowski Jr. had never felt more like his dad than he did after his father had died. He kept hearing his dad's music in his head. He had idolized Crazy Ray and had followed him out to Los Angeles instead of staying with his mother, Carrie in Wisconsin. That seemed light years ago, but being confined to a window seat on a jet from LAX to MKE created a space for contemplation. Being above the clouds and the troubles of earth gives perspective and perspective was the keyword today. In the seat directly behind him was Crazy's grieving girlfriend, Marcia. Somewhere in the baggage compartment was Crazy himself, now ashes in a guitar-shaped urn. Somewhere, down below and out there was Melanie Costello. Irish name, Asian beauty.

Before their brief meeting a few days before, Ray had been determined to concentrate on law school and not get distracted. Being a rock star's kid had given him lots of early experience with women, but in a way it was not real world experience. Even as a teenager, he knew that backstage was mostly a place where predators and wanna-be's competed for his dad's attention. What better way to get it than to dote on his kid. Somehow, Ray had managed to maneuver himself away from most of the drugs and sex, but not entirely. Someone named Jessica had gotten in under the radar.

Jessica—the mere passing of her name across his mind made him shudder. He had heard his father refer to her as 'living, breathing sex.' Of course a sixteen year old kid was interested. But when your first dose of love is cut from the cheapest part of the heart, it can be damaging. In Ray's case, she had taken him to bed and then made a joke of it: one which she shared with everyone. Looking back, it was a turning point. To avoid the snickers and lewd looks from his dad's friends, he somehow got serious about school. He never took one guitar lesson, either. His choice. Crazy Ray seemed disappointed at first, but then became a proud parent when the grades and honors began to come in. As the son's fine dominoes fell against the father's poor ones, things began to change in both of them. Life in the fast lane began to slow gradually. Then Crazy got sick and the prime of his career ended along with his health. It was the all too usual ending for this type of story: Fame followed fortune, followed fun, followed addictions, followed failure, followed remorse, followed by a puff of smoke, followed by nothing.

Ray's eyes came open and he realized he had been sleeping. He was a little embarrassed that his own snore might have awakened him. He glanced out the window and saw the southern ranges of Rocky Mountains with the high country still deep in spring snow. It was beautiful and peaceful. He decided at that moment that because of whom he was and where he came from that he could not allow even a hint of Hollywood seduction to ever be whispered behind his and Melanie's back. She was too young, too sweet: too perfect to make any move on. He knew she was not going to like the things he was going to tell her in a few hours. But then he wasn't going to like speaking them, either.

The jet roared out over the plains, now finding a beacon that was tracking it into General Mitchell Field. Ray turned around and smiled at Marcia. She smiled bravely back at him. He then laid his head against the window and dropped quickly into a dream within a dream.

Melanie wanted to go to the airport with Pat, but her mother needed her at home. In the great Wisconsin tradition of preparing food for grieving people, Molly was baking up a storm to take over to Pat's house for after the memorial service. There was also a rumor floating in the air that Carrie and Mike were coming in for the service. That would be great for Pat and for the girls. Mel only wanted to see the living Ray. She pictured him homing in not only for his dad, but for her. It was a sweet and exhilarating notion; one she knew was not real. But then fantasy by nature is not real. In her case it was a love story only a few pages into the plot. Beyond her bookmark, there were no printed words, only blank pages waiting to be graced.

"How much sugar again, Mom?"

"Just a half cup is all...blend it slowly into the butter and egg, honey"

Melanie began to stir and then suddenly slammed the spatula down on the counter causing a white cloud of crystals to rise. "I can't do this, Mom."

Molly looked at Melanie and saw rare anguish in her daughter's eyes. She was pretty sure where it came from. She had seen it often enough in her own reflection lately.

"Okay, tell you what. Let's both take a break from this."

Melanie's shoulders slumped, partly in relief and partly in shame. "I just feel so stupid making cakes. It's not my idea of chemistry."

"No, your idea of chemistry is whatever is going on between you and Ray."

"Mom."

"Yeah, it's me, Mom. Listen I have my own romantic anxiety going on right now, too. Okay? When I feel like this, I want to stay busy. What do you want to do, Mel?"

Melanie hung her head. "I want to be at Pat's when he gets there," she whispered.

"And what? Do you plan to go over there empty-handed?"

A light bulb blazed in Melanie's expansive brain. "I bring a cake?"

Molly nodded and smiled. Melanie picked up the flour sifter once more.

"One half cup, right?"

"Blended into the butter and egg, sweetie...gently."

CHAPTER TWENTY-FIVE

I watched a Red-tailed Hawk stoop onto a rabbit in the backyard today. There are a lot of Red-tails around here, but I never saw a raptor kill before and I am almost ashamed to say it was an event of great beauty. It was so pure and practiced that it had to be admired. I have seen humans swoop in on the meat department at the Pig and snatch meat with much less grace. Okay, bad analogy, but I couldn't resist. Anyway, while this hawk mantled its kill and began to snip at the rabbit fur, a crow landed nearby. Then there was another crow—and another. Soon I counted eight black crows standing in a circle around the hawk just watching and waiting for their shot at seconds. It was like a Far Side cartoon without the caption. Maybe it didn't need one. The humor was subtle, but it was in there. When I walked out into the yard, the crows looked at me, but did not budge. The hawk did not stop ripping. I quickly realized I was intruding on a ritual. I had walked into the wrong church and quickly went back into the house. I got one smug 'caw' honoring my departure.

Whenever Owen flashed in Molly's mind she found herself at the computer re-reading that last email from him. It was short and simple, but Molly read a million things into it. He said: I am back in Madison getting some work done on my face. I can't believe I am typing this to you, Molly. Please forgive me for not following up on our coffee date. I will call when I can. Owen.

Molly was pissed off. Apparently Mr. Wonderful didn't know his role. He was supposed to be thinking only of her; courting her, sweeping her off her feet. Damned men! She stormed back into the kitchen and was about to slap a towel against the oven door when the house phone rang. It rarely did these days. It was Harry Stompe.

"Molly?"

"Yes, hello, Harry." Her tone was somewhere between surprise and chill.

"Hey, I may be reading you wrong, but you sound pissed off. What's up?"

Molly slumped into a chair at the kitchen table and crossed her legs. It only took her a second to quickly thank God for Harry's timing. "Yeah, I was, but hearing your voice is the cup of kindness I needed. How are you, darling?"

"That's better. Haven't been called darling in years. You wanna dump it on me, Mol?"

"Oh, I don't know, Harry, just some more of my mid-life crisis crapola, I guess. What's on your mind?"

Harry paused for a second and Molly could hear him swallow. She guessed it was his nightly brandy.

"Well, when last we spoke, you got me all excited about this business with Roland's wife. Have you gotten a story for me yet?'

This time it was Molly who took the extra moment to inhale and exhale a sigh. "Harry, there isn't going to be a story."

"Oh?

"How can I explain this? Harry, Karin is a sweetheart. We sat down a couple days ago and she told me everything that happened between her and Roland leading up to their split up and…"

"And what?"

"And I decided not to make it public." The sentence hung on the nine hundred mile long line.

"May I ask why? Is it too sordid or too mundane?"

"It is both and neither. I just can't write it is all."

"I see."

"I can tell by your voice that you can't see. You're disappointed."

"Of course I am. As I told you before, anything biographical about Roland's early years is important to a lot of people. It's simple academics, Molly. The man is studied. His works are pored over in universities around the world. Any insight into his life is a nugget of gold. If you have some secrets, the

literary world wants them. And I want to give them that information through my magazine. Isn't that the way to look at it?"

"Actually, Harry you answered your own question."

"What?"

"It's a *family* secret and that's how it will stay."

"But, Molly dearest, you said you wanted to write this
story."

"I did, but I forgot one very important thing."

"Yes?"

"I am part of the family now, Harry. In every sense Karin
is my kin. She was willing to tell me her story if I helped her
get her sister back. We were strangers when the deal was
struck."

"But, strangers no more," Harry sighed.

"No. We are family," said Molly.

Again she heard the sound of a swallow on the other end.

"I should have realized that. Sorry. But can you scribble
something down about bratwurst or black and white cows for
me. I have some space to fill for the next issue."

"Harry, I will write you something very nice. Perhaps a
nice piece on ceramic deer."

"Deer?"

"Watch your email in say, three days. I gotta get off and
get some stuff out of the oven."

"I am defeated then?"

"You're so full of shit, Harry Stompe. Nothing ever
defeated you."

"God love you, Molly Costello…you and your damned
family."

"Finish your brandy. I'll write you something good."

"Goodnight, Mol"

"Goodnight. I love you."

The oven timer went off with a cheerful ding and Molly's
mood never returned to the place it was before the phone call.
Before she took the last cake out of the oven something caught
her eye. It was a slip of paper sticking out of one of Sonia's
books, a bookmark perhaps. It was Sony's handwriting that

caught her eye and the first line had made her want to read the rest. She slipped the paper out and read:

Do you applaud with silence
The movement of a million wings
In colors unimagined
A harmony of heartstrings
Rare as air on the moon
But, very soon from afar
I fly to my home, Darfur

All Molly could do was mouth a silent 'Wow!'

The author of the poem was standing just outside the Fond du Lac Public Library waiting with her friend Martha for their ride to Pipe. Martha's mom was running a little late, but the night was warm and it felt good to stand and stretch after a couple hours of research and homework.

"So, have you heard from him at all yet then?" Martha asked just to pass the time.

"Him?"

"You know who."

"Oh, Hector. No, but I didn't expect him to write or call," said Sonia, now wishing the ride would come quickly. Talking about Hector might turn this night sad.

"Why?"

"Because it's better this way, that's why. We were friends is all."

"You liked him, Sonia. You said you guys kissed."

Sonia now turned to her friend quickly to close off a thread that might unravel into tears.   "Marty, kissing isn't everything. He taught me things about life and was my friend. We were never going to be together for long. He was always going back to Mexico and I was always going…" Sonia cut herself off. Her vision of the future was still half hidden from the world.

"Where? Where are you going?"

Just then Martha's mom pulled up and the side door to a mini van slowly opened automatically.

"Home," said Sonia and she dove into the back of the van.

Dr. Owen Palmer was not ignoring Molly Costello because he didn't care about her. The fact of the matter was that he could not get her out of his mind. But then his attraction to her had an equal and opposite reaction; he considered himself an unsuitable suitor. When he got back to Long Lake after his face work, he sat down at his desk and made another very careful assessment of the damages to his practice. He learned for a fact what he had suspected, he no longer had clients and he was falling into debt. Sometimes women do not understand that when a man cannot provide well, he cannot love well. Owen understood this from studying his beloved animals. The strong and prosperous males took the females and the weak just trotted along behind the pack. To add to this, he no longer felt attractive. He took a sneak peek into his future and saw nothing good on the horizon. How could he bring Molly into this world? She seemed to be attracted to him, he thought, but he knew in his heart it would all go sour quickly. What if they did hook up? Eventually she would have to make concessions to his failure. He could not allow this.

And so those metaphoric walls began to be erected by the masons of pride. He decided to shut it all down for a while. He knew Molly would be hurt, which made him hurt, but it was all going to be for her, anyway. A gift of tough love or some stupid thing like that. He headed off to Kewaskum to get some groceries, which would allow him to lay low just long enough to lose her. On the way to the store, he passed the Jersey Flats Kame and pulled over on the side of CTH G and stared at it. Why had she mentioned a 'kame' the last time he saw her?

In what he thought was the final act of his relationship with Molly, Owen got out of his car and began to walk across the prairie towards the mound of rock and trees in the center of the field. As he walked he discovered that the kame was farther away than it looked. The prairie grass was high and wet with morning dew and his unexercised legs began to cramp. He almost turned his ankle a couple times in hidden holes. He stumbled over rocks lurking deep in the grass. When he got to the base of the mound, he looked for an approach and saw something like a worn pathway to the top. It looked like it hadn't been visited in a long time, but at least it showed him the way to the top.

At the summit, he did a quick 360 degree reconnoiter. To the west was his car parked on the road and behind that a thick forest that he knew was cut by the Zillmer Trail. To the south was what looked to be old church converted into a house and its attending graveyard. To the east a ridgeline of trees rose above New Prospect, and the view to the north was dominated by Dundee Mountain with a horse ranch in the foreground. The kame itself had mere grass on the north side and a few stunted trees grew on the south. He found a likely rock and sat down in the exact center of his universe and began to think. He did not move for a peaceful hour. And then another hour went by.

By midmorning a storm front was coming in fast and dark from the west and he could smell the rain. It was the third week in May now and the storms were already tropical and dramatic. Owen hurried to his car and, forgetting the groceries, headed for home. The wall cloud passed over him just as he reached his rickety garage. He pulled in and closed the door. With nothing else to do that day, he picked up a pen and a crossword puzzle and turned a light on next to the couch. In minutes the sound of the rain on the roof and the morning darkness put him to sleep.

Crazy Ray Hitowski's health had been in decline for some time and somewhere along the way he wrote the script for his end. Besides the guitar-shaped urn (Fender Stratocaster, of course) he dictated that he would be buried in Fond du Lac, but not before a goodbye party was thrown for his family and friends. Surprisingly, about thirty people came in from L.A. along with some rock and roll beat writers. The local throng got the word and the attendee list was around one hundred in total. What was left of the Fond du Lac Hitowski's put their heads together with Pat Stouffer and they managed to secure a roller skating arena at the last minute for the event. Crazy had also arranged to pay for the party, which was good because the Hitowski's and Stouffer's were not prepared for his list of requests.

The memorial party would be catered by Shaeffer's, the oldest restaurant in town and the menu consisted of Crazy's favorites from his youth: ham loaf and spare ribs with sauerkraut. Kegs of beer were ordered and a tap bar was set up early in the afternoon. The funeral instructions said Pabst Blue Ribbon and no other. A local band was hired, one that did Crazy Ray covers and somehow they came up with a strobe light show that was showing its age, but functional. Ray Jr. threw his dad's money at the skating rink management and they handled the rest. Despite the morning thunderstorm, the party was set to go off at 4PM. The folks who wandered into the bizarre location shook their heads and commented that Crazy would have loved this mess. The only thing missing was the clergy. A pastor or a priest might have attended the bacchanal, but none were invited. Crazy's request, of course.

Melanie was respectful of Ray Jr.'s duties, and while she stayed close by, she did not smother him as she would like to. Ray told her they would talk later and that sounded reasonable. Maybe.

With the rink filled with happy mourners, the party began precisely at four with the national anthem done Hendrix style. After that it was beer, food, and music. Before people got too wild in their grieving, Ray grabbed the mike and asked for their attention. He got it.

"Hello, everyone. As you may or may not know I am Crazy Ray's son, Ray Jr."

Someone yelled out, "Not-so Crazy Ray!" And everyone laughed.

"Yes," Ray went on. "I just wanted to take a minute or two to read you something that my dad wrote a few weeks before he died. He told Marcia he wanted me to read it here today."

Suddenly the rink got quiet despite the acoustics that amplified every burp. The gathering sensed that Crazy was going to speak to them from the urn, which is exactly what he was doing. Ray cleared his throat and read the paper, which was handwritten on a yellow legal pad, just as all of Crazy's lyrics had been:

Hey, everyone, I'm dead. Okay, don't cheer too loud. But, don't cry either. I had a pretty sweet life and probably did everything I could think of to make this day come earlier than later. The fact is, I thought of death the first time I ever stood in front of an audience that loved my music. I thought that if I died right then, it was okay. I had got my foot on the first rung of the rock and roll ladder and there was nowhere to go but up and then eventually over. I lived the life I had dreamed about in my bedroom here in Fondy when I practiced my playing in front of a poster of Jimi Hendrix. Anyway, I knew going in that Jimi was dead and many of my contemporaries probably wished they were. A funny thing happens when you figure out that you have a little talent; it goes to your head in the form of drugs, drink, and sex. I knew it all and did it anyway. So don't cry for me fucking Argentina. Right now while you guys are partying in my hometown, I am far away. I'm either in Heaven with my family, friends, idols, and dogs or I am in Hell learning banjo. After today forget me. I only wish you peace.

It took a few moments for everyone to understand that Ray was done speaking. Someone started to clap and everyone else joined in. The band started playing Crazy's signature song, *Fuck the Planet* and the party shifted back into high. Some of the older folks, a few relations just shook their heads and made excuses to wander off, but Crazy Ray's party troopers would stay until the beer was gone around midnight.

Melanie and Ray peeled themselves away around 10PM and walked back to Pat's house. The sidewalks were still wet and the town was quiet. There was silent, golden lightning off to the north. When they got to Pat's, the garage was open and in the dim back light they could see two people were sitting out in Bim's fortress taking in the warm night. As they got closer, Melanie recognized both people. Ray only knew one of them, but he knew her well.

"Hi, Mom. You missed the party," he said.

A voice that Ray had not heard very often over the years said, "Hello Ray. And hello beautiful Melanie. We got held up by bad weather between here and Boston."

Melanie was already getting a big hug from Mike Gabler. "Oh Mike and Carrie, I've missed you guys." She broke off with Mike and she and Carrie Stirling bear-hugged.

Just then Pat turned on the back porch light and came out all smiles. "You two recognize these kids? Molly and Sony are in the house. Come on in everyone."

Mike, who had known Ray's dad, held out a hand." Hello, Ray, I'm Mike." They shook hands.

"My god, Melanie, you are all grown up," said Carrie. As she spoke she took note that her son's eyes were adoring Melanie. Even in the semi-darkness, she recognized an attraction. This was going to be an interesting couple of days in Fond du Lac.

The group ambled into the house where they found Molly and Sonia sitting at the big and seldom used dining room table having cake and coffee. Everyone settled into a seat and the catch-up and gentle conversations began. Only a few of the local Hitowski's had shown up there for dessert and they had gone home early. That was fine with Pat. This was the group she wanted around her table. Even Bim was still up and sitting at the table's head. He waved a hand to his wife.

"You close the garage door, Patsy?"

Pat nodded in the affirmative. Bim smiled and Pat beamed.

CHAPTER TWENTY-SIX

Somehow I dreamed about the cougar last night. I remembered very little of that dream, but it had me up with my coffee in the morning doing research on my computer in the studio. What astounded me the most was the fact that these three cats walked all the way from the Black Hills in South Dakota with one of them veering off and causing major changes in several people's lives. Of course, Owen was its worst victim, but so was I. And it was my dream, for cry-eye. I brooded for several minutes thinking about crumby hands dealt by fickle fate. I almost missed the point. We live on a planet shared by many species. We are the smartest of the bunch, but maybe a little too smart sometimes. I have no doubt that is was some act of man that sent those cats away from their natural habitat and put them on their alien course. The exact act that did this will never be known, but when something wild comes into our backyards it usually isn't there because it wants to be. I can swallow that, but to have a cougar travel so far to attack a veterinarian on a recreational trail is tragic irony that only Shakespeare could even contemplate. The next time you haunt my bedroom, Roland, whisper the answer to me.

"So you expect me to sit in a car for four days?" Meg Bollander knew the simple answer was 'yes,' but she knew she needed to put up some slight outrage if only out of habit. The fact was, the deal was done. For the first time in her life, she was leaving the state of Wisconsin and heading out across the country. This greatest adventure of her life was to begin in only three days.

"You can ride shotgun, Meg," said Leah. "I saw the whole thing on the way out."

"What whole thing?" asked Meg. They were out in her yard cleaning it up for the first time in ages, picking up branches and bits of wind-blown garbage.

"America," shouted Karin. "You get to see your country. You get to see more scenes to paint, Sissy."

"Hrumph!" Meg grunted, but actually the idea was blooming within her mind. "We gonna see mountains? Ain't never seen one, you know."

"We are going to cross the mountains...lots of them," said Karin, smiling at her sister's naïveté.

"And anytime you want to hop out and set up your easel, we can do that," Leah added. It was no secret that she couldn't wait to see Meg in action and aiming her talent at something besides Lake Winnebago.

"Well, I don't know about that," said Meg, but she knew. Whatever the artistic worm was that had eaten into the apple of her heart, it was hungry for more than its usual diet. This desire caused a funny feeling, almost as pleasant as an Old Fashioned buzz.

Molly had helped Meg find a man who would look after her place for a couple months, and after a long interview, Meg had agreed to the deal. As a sweetener, Leah had already purchased seven oils for what Meg thought was an astounding price. She was suddenly wealthy by her modest standards and that was something new, too.

"This world is sure spinning fast," Meg whispered to herself.

"What was that?" asked her sister.

"Oh, nothing. I was just thinking that I might be getting happy. The notion makes me dizzy."

Leah started twirling around with a branch in her hand like a magic wand and shouting, "Woo hoo!" Karin mimicked Leah and then slowly, as though the accelerator pedal had been pushed on a glacier, Meg Bollander began to twirl around in a circle, too. This was the sublime moment of the official reconciliation of the Bollander sisters. They were suddenly young again as they were before the time of Roland. The future was now beyond Winnebago and no longer bounded by its far shoreline.

Molly and Mike Gabler had not had a chance to talk privately the night of Crazy Ray's memorial party. The glances they had exchanged indicated to both of them that such a chat was necessary. Carrie knew this, too, and made a date with Pat, Sonia and Melanie to go to lunch the next day. Since Ray Jr. was tied up with the last details of paying for and cleaning up the event, Melanie accepted Carrie's invite without feeling as if she were burning Ray's short amount of time in town. Their tete a tete would come later that night, anyway. Besides Mel, Sony was dying to know everything about Mike and Carrie's life in Massachusetts, their almost forgotten former home state. Everyone split up to talk.

"We've got to stop meeting at funerals." Mike quipped sitting across the table from Molly at the Bagelmeister. It was only half a joke. Molly smiled, but she was a little distracted since she had not been in the place since the last time she had seen Owen, or JB for that matter.

"Hey, Molly, you in there?"

Molly recovered quickly. "Sorry, I was thinking about something, someone else."

"Roland?"

"I think about him every day, but it was someone I was here with a couple weeks ago."

"Must be a boyfriend. You've got that look," said Mike.

Molly's smile became quizzical. "That look? You and I have known each other for five years or so, but we only spent one week together. Since when do you become an expert on 'my look?'?"

"Molly, that was such an intense week back then that we are forever going to know each other as well as we know ourselves. You gonna tell me what's eating you?"

The coffee shop suddenly became a confessional. "His name is Owen. I found him and lost before I could blink an eye. How does that happen, Mike? I mean it was so intense and then poof."

"Who is this guy? Am I going to have to beat him up?"

A smile flirted across Molly's face as she remembered how Mike had decked Crazy Ray once for Carrie's honor. "I don't think so. He's a veterinarian. I met him when the owl died. We sort of had some instant bond, but then things happened. It's a long story, but I miss him, Mike." Molly's voice cracked like a heart-shaped egg.

"How far had this relationship gone, Mol?"

She shook her head emphatically. "Nothing like that. It was just emotional…intensely emotional."

"And he felt the same way?"

"I thought so. Now I don't know. He is cutting me out completely. No phone calls, no emails, not even a freaking text message. I even drove over to where he lives and he won't answer the door. Except, I know he's there. Lights at night."

"I'm sorry, Molly." Mike reached over and took her hand. She looked at his hand and then cocked her head. There was a gold ring on the proper finger.

"Oh my god, Mike! How long?"

"About three weeks ago."

"But, what, you didn't tell anyone?"

Mike rocked back on his chair as he fidgeted with his coffee cup. "We kept it low key for professional reasons. It's hard to explain without sounding cocky, but some of my models like to flirt when they pose. It's part of the game. Carrie knows that. She assists me on most of my shoots. We decided to leak it out slowly that we are married."

"God, I hope you leaked it to Pat."

"Actually, Pat has known since the day of the marriage."

Molly's eyebrows soared upward. "She knew? She kept a secret? From me?"

"Carrie made her promise. Bim, too. Anyway, now you know."

Molly's tears shifted from sadness to joy as she stood up and grabbed Mike around the head like a wrestler, almost pulling him off his chair. "That's the best thing I have heard in weeks. Oh, congratulations. We have to celebrate. Can I tell the girls?"

"Carrie is telling them probably as we speak."

And indeed, she was over lunch in another part of town.

Owen had gotten into the daily habit of visiting Jersey Flats. It gave him the space and breathing room he needed to think. Lee Krieger had called and told him about a vet over in Beaver Dam who was looking for an associate. It would mean the total abandonment of the Long Lake practice, but it was beyond repair anyway. He pondered the move. It seemed logical. Lee said he had to move on it by the end of the month, which was only days away now. Owen looked for answers as he meditated on the shape of Dundee Mountain.

It had been a week or so since Molly had come to his place and rattled the door. He wanted to break down and let her in, but he had calculated the trajectory of their relationship too often. Maybe if he got re-established in Beaver Dam, they might date or something. He knew deep down that would never happen if he left the area. He could only reach out to Molly through her books. He had finished *Silent Silos* and was now a hundred or so pages into *Melting Earth*. He heard her voice in the words, but there was another voice that came across into his subconscious. It was a masculine voice booming between the lines; a voice both soothing and angry. Owen was enough of a reader to know who it was and tried to ignore it. Few readers could ignore Roland Heinz for long. A passage from *Melting Earth* led him to that conclusion:

Logan endured the winter like a prisoner promised parole. He knew the game was a battle and the battle was his sanity. When the snow turned dirty and the geese again stirred up the low gray sky he stopped putting red x's on the calendar and walked out into the yard. He closed his eyes and allowed his great nose to find the scent of hope. He sampled the damp air and first tasted the old snow, breaking down not to the sun, but to the temperatures above freezing. He urged his sensory digestion to dig deeper, filtering out the almost constant odor of excrement from the Holsteins. He held his breath; maybe today was not the day. But then, in the instant before he opened his eyes, he sorted it all out and found it: the sweet, almost sexual smell of melting earth. He drew breath greedily now, and thought about his plow. The smell of fertile soil awakening meant that he would now return to Heaven for the sixty-ninth time in the fields of his father.

He closed the book quickly, placing the marker carefully knowing he never wanted to finish Molly's book. But the pages were numbered.

When Melanie came through the kitchen door at Ghost Farm later that night, she found Sonia sitting alone at the table studying for her finals. Sonia studied her sister's face knowing that she had just come from having her long talk with Ray. Melanie got a soda out of the fridge and plunked down. The pop-top snapped and hissed. Sonia was all eyes and ears.

"Where's Mom?" asked Mel.

"She's out with Carrie, Mike, and Pat celebrating the wedding."

"What do you think about that?"

"I think it's great. What about you?"

"I think it is, too, but the secrecy was a little weird."

"Well, it's not a secret anymore," Sonia noted.

"I suppose." Melanie was warming up to something.

"So…?" It was the trigger question of the night. Sony waited as Mel took a quick swallow of her soda and then hiccupped. She had rehearsed her reply a little.

"The age thing is not that important. The geographical thing is huge, but we will stay in touch daily and get together when we can. The school thing, our careers, is what is most important now and we should give that most of our attention."

"His words?"

"Yes, but I know he is right."

"What about love? Do you guys love each other?"

Melanie shook her head. "It's not love yet, sis." Mel startled herself with this statement.

"You sound so business-like."

"Umm. Well, there's sort of two levels to this. He and I are both kind of cool on the outside, but there is definitely something doing flips on the inside."

"He told you that?"

"In a way…"

Melanie took her can and began to walk into the living room. "I need to check my email."

"Melanie! What way?"

Mel turned around and gave her sister an exaggerated smile as she crossed her eyes. "He kissed me again. And this time it was movie kiss, Sony!" she said as she spun into the other room. Sonia leapt up and followed her.

"Details!"

CHAPTER TWENTY-SEVEN

My yellow barn is bright on the outside, but dark and forbidding on the inside. It is an aging structure that began to die when the last drop of milk was taken many years ago. The owl had kept it alive for a while, bringing Roland and my owl-watching children in to daydream, but when the owl died, it seemed all life departed. One day I sat for a full hour in Roland's folding chair and didn't hear so much as a mouse or pigeon rustle in the gloom. The girls had not been out here in ages. I felt like the barn was a metaphor for my heart—big and empty. My first instinct was to leave and never come back. I would close it up forever. But then, from out of nowhere, I heard a voice in my head telling me to open it up and fill it with new light. Again, the voice was unmistakable. As always, when my crazy emotional compass stopped spinning, its needle pointed due north to the memory of my adoptive father. An idea was hatching as a mourning dove called from the roof. I was not alone after all.

Bim Stouffer was enjoying an especially warm late May morning in the garage when he saw Molly's little Subaru park in front of the house. He figured she'd be over early to do a rehash of the week once she knew about Carrie's wedding and Ray had flown back to Los Angeles leaving her daughter spinning like a top. Yes, thought Bim, you see it all from the garage, but nobody understood that but him. He expected Molly to go in the front door and avoid him, but by gosh, she was heading right at him with a 'let's talk' look on her face.

"G'day, Molly. You have a determined look today."

Molly nodded and kept striding until she sat down in the lawn chair next to Bim. "I just got off the phone with Pat and she said you had some news for me. Cough it up."

"Oh that." Now Bim knew he was in control of the situation. He had forgotten that little bit of information that he had told Pat the night before. He cracked open a beer and offered one to Molly. She refused, as he expected. She wanted information, not hops.

"Yeah, well I was down at Fleet Farm last night and ran into your friend, Owen Palmer. I kinda knew the guy cuz we bowled together once, but I barely recognized him what with the scars and such."

"Go on."

"So, I hailed him down. Told him who I was and all that. Said I was a friend of yours. Hope that was okay, Molly."

"We are friends, Bim…for now."

Now Bim was feeling the light of interrogation and needed a gulp in order to proceed. "Okay, listen, I was looking out for you is all. I told him he shouldn't have dropped you like a twice-baked potato and maybe he should give you a call or something."

Molly was horrified and yet deeply interested in the narrative. "I'm guessing he told you to bug off."

"Not at all. In fact he pulled me into a quiet aisle…think it was plumbing fixtures and we had a nice man to man talk."

"You're shitting me, right?"

"No." Bim leaned into Molly. "I think he wanted to talk to someone who knew you." Bim winked.

Molly thought, Jesus Christ, I can't get the man to answer the phone and then he is talking about me to the King of Garages in the plumbing aisle at Fleet Farm. "Go on, Bim," she said.

"Look, Molly, he's a real nice guy. He told me his business is gone bust and he is taking a job in Beaver Dam. He told me he couldn't afford to date you and…"

"Date me? We had coffee once!"

"Let me finish, okay. That's his line, but the Bimster hasn't been around this long without knowing a little bit about how guys really feel. This guy thinks he is doing you a favor, Molly. He thinks he is saving you from pitying him and maybe loathing yourself for doing it. He thinks he is being noble. In short, I think he *is* in love with you."

"Doesn't sound too much like love to me."

"You still don't understand these Cheesehead guys, Mol. Pride is a big thing. What do you think we hide behind the stupid Packers for? Why do you think we are all the mighty hunters and back-slapping bar buddies? It's pride. Pride and the fact that women scare the shit out of us. We try to read your minds all the time, but all we are reading is our own preconceived ideas of what we think you are thinking. Trust me, this man is in love…and I got proof."

The proof part threw Molly. "What proof?"

"Well," Bim began and drew the thought out with another hit on the beer can. "I just happened to notice he was carrying one of your books. A paperback of that Melting thing whatever it's called. I noticed it was worn like he had been reading it over and over. It had a bookmark in it with an owl on it."

Molly stared at Bim. She couldn't talk. His powers of observation more than surprised her. Somehow this last piece of information struck a chord.

"Take it for what it's worth, girl. In this town if a guy is carrying a girl's book in his hand he is carrying the girl in his heart."

Suddenly, Molly saw Bim in a new light. My god, was there a poet in the garage sitter? More importantly, was he right?

"I have to go talk to Pat. Thanks for telling me this, Bim."

"Only have your best interests at heart, Mol."

Molly then did something she never thought she would do. She stood up and kissed Bim on the top of his head. "You and I *are* friends, Bimster." And she meant it.

Meg Bollander crossed the Continental Divide just west of Rawlins, Wyoming. Leah explained to her that from here on the big rivers drained off into the Pacific Ocean. For some reason this fact astounded Meg. It was a previously unconsidered thing, which seemed to burst the dam that had held back her curiosity for her entire life. Now everything was interesting. Before they left Wisconsin, Karin had given her sister a very fine digital camera to record the trip and once Meg had mastered it, she had pointed it at almost everything that caught her eye. This meant that the women had to make many frequent stops, but it was worth it to watch Meg in artistic action. One stop was on Utah Rt. 66 as they cut the corner between I-80 and I-84 in the Wasatch Mountains east of Salt Lake City.

Meg found herself for the first time in a winding canyon, flushed by spring snow melt and alive with birds. When she got out of the car, she stood and stared up at the cliffs like they were tall buildings.

"Well, look at this!" she shouted as Karin and Leah stretched on the roadside. "Look at all the people in the rocks. Karin, you see them?"

Karin and Leah smiled and squinted, but didn't quite see what Meg was talking about. Meg walked over between them.

"Look right there. See the mother with her two kids. And behind her...an old man bent with age." She drew out her camera and began to shoot. When she was finished with a dozen shots, Meg handed the camera to Leah, who scanned the shots through the viewing window on the back of the camera.

"Holy cow, I see them now!" Leah looked from the camera back to the rocks. "I see them."

"Let me look," said Karin. Meg handed the camera to her. "Oh yeah."

"I'm gonna paint this when we get to your place, sis," Meg declared.

Karin was surprised and relieved. She thought Meg was going to want to set up the easel right there and begin. "You can paint from the pictures?"

Meg grinned as she took a few more shots across the road. "Hah, what is a camera, but a little boost to the memory, Karin. I don't need to be looking at something to paint it; I just need to see it in my head. This camera will help with the shape and color, but it won't quite come out of me the way it comes out of the camera. It helps, though. My memory ain't what it used to be." Then she paused for a long moment and sighed adding, "Thank God."

Farther west on I-80 as they crossed the salt flats west of Salt Lake City, Meg once again made Karin stop so she could admire the vast expanse broken only by distant mountains.

"This must be what the moon looks like," said Meg.

"We came through here in the dark on the way out and I never noticed all the graffiti," Leah noted. Near the road people had arranged various rocks, bottles, and cans into words and designs that were probably more easily read from the air.

"People like to make themselves immortal," Karin said as she strained to read one name. "Hey, look Leah." She pointed to a bottle arrangement that said: *Leah Holt-SLC*.

"Neat," said Leah, "although I might have preferred rocks to beer bottles."

While Karin and Leah were giggling Meg had wandered off a ways onto the salt flat with her camera. She had found a flower design of painted pebbles. The girls caught up with her. "This took some planning," noted Meg. "They gathered the rocks and painted them first. They knew what they wanted to do before they got here." She composed a picture and then sighed. "This is as far away from Wisconsin as you can get. Not a tree or a hill in sight. No cows, no barns, no churches, no taverns. I *am* standing on the moon."

"You getting homesick, sis?" asked Karin.

Meg looked off at the horizon and then squinted up into the sky. She shoved her camera into her pocket and faced her traveling companions. She then smiled like she had been tickled. "Always wanted to see the moon."

Karin was looking at her sister in a very different light these days and that light was blinding. Neither of them were spring chickens anymore, but Meg had been suppressed for so long that now that she had awakened everything that came out of her mouth or out through her brush hand was amazing. And if there was a notion that most of her life had been wasted, Karin knew she had contributed mightily to that fact. But, enlightenment can come late in life and it is a miracle at any age. Karin found herself smiling at every one of Meg's observations. It was like she was seeing the world for the first time through Meg's long sequestered eyes.

"You ready to move on, sis?" Karin asked.

"Yes I am," Meg answered as they all head back to the car. "Let's get out of here. These Mormons wouldn't know an Old Fashioned from a glass of piss."

There were more mountains and valleys ahead and then the Pacific Ocean. In Santa Barbara, several of Meg's paintings had already arrived at Leah's gallery, resting in their shipping crates and waiting to open up the whole wide world for their creator.

Owen continued to make the hike to the Jersey Flats kame a part of his daily routine. It gave him solitude without a roof. The hour or so of contemplation was the most relaxing part of the day and he cherished it. The Beaver Dam job ultimatum had been delayed an additional two weeks and that gave him a little more time to think about the logistics. It seemed like it was the best and only option, but it was also surrender and that made him uncomfortable. He would not be the boss anymore for one thing. For another, he would miss his home in Long Lake. He poured it over in his mind each day until he ascended the kame. From there he knew he had to move on.

On this gauzy sunlit morning just before Memorial Day he was thinking about his encounter with the man at Fleet Farm, who knew Molly. He wondered if and what information had gotten back to her. He knew what he told the man about not being able to date her sounded idiotic, even to himself. More than likely nothing would come of it. Molly had stopped calling, emailing, and had not come by the clinic except for that one time.

Owen wanted to move on, but he was riding a pile of boulders that had ridden a glacier at a faster speed than he could summon. He felt like the gravity at this place was a hundred times stronger than anywhere else he sat. Being lonely is to wear an anchor with a long chain. No matter where you go it finds the bottom and grabs it and stops your forward progress. Owen Palmer, DVM, was shackled to Jersey Flats. While he waited, he pulled a worn paperback book out of his shoulder bag and removed the owl bookmark. He searched those pages for instruction on how to weigh anchor and sail on.

Meg had quickly decided that she would stay at Leah's studio while she was visiting. There was a small apartment that Leah used from time to time that opened out onto patio above a garage. From that place Meg had a view of the Pacific Ocean, which had become her newest artistic fixation. When the days were clear, she had her easel set up and began what her sister called her 'California Period.' By any name it was producing more amazing oils. Apparently, Meg's talent was not left behind on The Ledge.

At her first in studio showing, Meg found she had a taste for fine California wines. Because she noticed people around there sipped instead of gulped, she slowly weaned herself off of the hard Midwestern libations and became somewhat moderate in her drinking. This did not in any way affect the quality of her work; it merely allowed her to work faster without the stupors.

After a month in California, Meg had settled into a routine that not only included painting, but lots of warm socializing with Karin, Leah, and some new friends interested in her art. There quickly developed a lightness of heart that was so new and pleasant that it had to be addressed.

"So, when am I supposed to go back to the farm again, Karin?" Meg wondered over lunch.

"There's no timetable, Sis. You can stay here as long as you like. I thought you knew that?"

Meg nodded and daintily sipped a glass of a local golden Chardonnay. She then dabbed her lips with her white cloth napkin. "What would you say if I didn't want to go back, Karin?"

Karin took this news in carefully. She had hoped something like this would happen, but didn't think Meg could ever cut ties to the farm and the lifestyle she had known her entire life. Her response required her to reach across the table and take her sister's hand.

"I would love it if you stayed here. Leah would love it, too, but I want you to be sure, Meg. Once you decide to move, there would be no going back. The farm will have to be sold, you know?"

"Hah, what farm?" Meg paused for effect. "You mean that place where I sat by myself for all those years hating the man who lived below me? You think I would be sentimental about that?"

"Maybe."

"Karin, when you and I were young, all the pretty girls left those winters and moved away to someplace warm…Florida or California. You did it a little later. Now I am going to do it a little later still. How many years do I have left, anyway? I decided I want to keep all of this and stay here. You're going to have to help me arrange it, you know. I don't know the first thing about selling property."

Karin though she would burst with happiness. This was the outcome she had dreamed of when she first conceived her plan to go back to Wisconsin. It amazed her that sometimes things in life worked out just perfectly. She instinctively pulled out her cell phone and called Leah as Meg listened.

"Hi, guess what? My sister is going to permanently join our coven. Yes! Can you call that realtor you know? Uh huh. We have a farm to list in Pipe, Wisconsin."

CHAPTER TWENTY-EIGHT

Summer is anticipated in Wisconsin like a wedding. It is a brief ceremony, warm and full of love and emotion. It is a rite, a festival, and a celebration of a promise that the waiting and lonely suffering of the nine month courtship is finally over and consummation will occur under a big, yellow moon. Blinding white legs are now in shorts. The long underwear and woolens are back in the cedar chest. The mud room boots are in a box in the basement and the flower baskets get watered instead of mourned. I love that kids still ride goofy old bikes around here for fun. I love that every small town is lit up by a night game at the ball field. I love that corn is more than knee high by the Fourth of July. Sitting outside in the evening with the fireflies and night birds is magical at this latitude because the afterglow of day lasts until around ten o'clock. In late August we notice the flocking of the birds and the yellow tips on the trees, but it was a fine wedding and the vows will be repeated next year.

Molly wasn't quite sure how to process the information that Bim had provided concerning his Owen sighting, but the news did have one very astounding side effect. She was writing again. Apparently the image of Owen Palmer walking around Fleet Farm clutching her book had broken the dam that was holding her creativity in check. Perhaps in the back of her mind she wanted to give him another book to read if she could not give him anything else. She was in the cheese shed studio early on this last day of May writing in a good and steady rhythm she had not known in months. The night before she had quickly reeled off the article that she had promised to Harry Stompe and had emailed it off to him. It was a piece about Roland after all, but it dealt mostly with the local geography of his novels. She and Melanie had gone on a quick field trip with a digital camera and had captured about three dozen pertinent pictures and Molly had given them words. Harry's one word reply to her filing was a simple, "Wow!"

The new novel was simply titled, *Holylands*. It was her third Wisconsin novel and it was turning into a love letter to the characters she had come to know and grown to love. The story was unspooling effortlessly. When she took a break to rest her fingers and finish her coffee, there was a soft rap on the door. Molly recognized Sonia's touch.

"Come in, Sony."

The door opened and revealed a smiling young woman who had just turned fourteen the day before. Her birthday gift was her own laptop and she had it under her arm as she entered the shed.

"Hi, Mom. You still writing away?"

"Com'ere once and sit." Sonia alit on the couch next to Molly. "You want a peek?"

Molly swiveled her laptop and Sony leaned in to read a couple paragraphs.

"Very cool. You are definitely back, Mom. This character sounds like Pat."

"Maybe it is, maybe it isn't."

"Well, I think it is."

"What do you have on your notebook? Anything I can peek at?"

Of course, that was why Sonia had carried her work with her. She was eager to show her mom what she had written that morning.

"Okay," Sonia said. She opened the lid and a page popped up. It was a poem. Poetry had become her medium of expression and poems were pouring out of her almost as fast as they were conceived in the mind. All of them were extraordinary. Molly read in silence:

It is not hard to find the prey
In their multi-colored tents
Drawn by food and sacraments
To escape the wind and hide
In a depression while the procession
Of Janjaweed raiders ride
The dusty roads of genocide

Molly handed the notebook back to Sonia. "This really is your life now, isn't it? You want to be the Poet Laureate of Darfur?" The thought both scared Molly and made her very proud.

"All I know is I want to help my people, Mom. I have to do something."

"I think that is good, honey, but do you know what a hard road you are setting yourself on?"

"Yes, and I know it is probably worse over there than I can even imagine."

"I'm sure it is. And it is going to be at least three years before you can get involved. I know you have researched the NGO's and UN efforts, but lots can change in that time. You know that, right?"

"Yes. But, I can use that time to prepare myself."

Molly could only look at her daughter and nod. Somehow she sensed that Sonia would not waver over time. "What will you do?"

"Well, for starters...I will become the Poet Laureate of Darfur."

"You might be already, babe. Where did all this come from? I feel like I missed something: some change in you over the last couple months."

Sonia's face softened into a smile that was borderline angelic. "It was Hector, mom. Do you remember the day he and I went out to pick up stones in the farmer's field with the other Mexican workers?"

Molly nodded.

"Well, that was the day I changed. Those men broke their backs to send a few dollars home to their families. It made me think about where I came from. I love my life here, Mom, and this is not me rebelling against anything. This is home, but I have two of them and one of them is suffering."

Molly put her arm around Sonia and pulled her in close for a squeeze. "I understand, okay? During the next few years you let me know what I can do to help you." They both were letting a couple of love tears out when Melanie came through the door.

"What's wrong?" asked Mel, who was slightly alarmed by the scene.

"Nothing's wrong, Mel," Molly sniffled. "We are just having a mother-daughter moment."

Melanie walked over and sat down on the couch on the other side of Molly. She had a sheet of printed paper in her hand that Molly glanced at. "Are you writing now, too?"

Melanie looked at the paper and smiled. "No, someone else wrote it and I printed it. Mom, I just got my first love letter." She handed it to her Mom as Sonia leaned in to read it, too.

Molly quickly read it and handed it back.

"It's not mushy or anything," said Mel, "but it's just right. It sounds like Ray...the way he talks and all. What do you think?"

"I think you've found a nice guy, Mel," said Molly.

"But he's so far away," said Sonia.

Melanie stood up and smiled with her eyes closed. She held up the printed email page and waved it like a flag. "He's right here. I'm holding him in my hand. I'm going back in the house and put myself in his hand. That's how it's going to work for now."

Before Melanie left the shed, she turned around with an afterthought. "I almost forgot. Mom, Liz Schmidt called and left a message on the house line. She wants to know if you want to go horseback riding this morning. And there was a call from Karin, too."

"Okay, I'm coming in."

Molly hadn't been on a horse for years, but Liz had asked her to ride a couple times before and she had turned her down. Maybe this was the day to get out and do something different. It sure felt that way. Karin's call was left over from earlier. Molly already knew about Meg's decision to remain in California. It was going to be strange not having Meg living above them on The Ledge, but Molly realized how healing it would be for both Bollander sisters to move on with their lives. Roland, more than anyone, would have liked this outcome.

When the three women of Ghost Farm left the studio and went into the house, there was a little gust of warm wind that blew in the window that faced east. It headed into the corner behind the wood-burning stove and picked up some flaky soot and spun it into a tiny funnel of black dust. As the little whirlwind lengthened, it caught a dry oak leaf and sent it into the air. When it came to rest it sat atop Molly's closed laptop on the coffee table. For just an instant the veins of the oak leaf shimmered with a faint blue glow. The glow pulsed several times and then faded away.

Liz Schmidt picked Molly up around ten o'clock in a truck pulling a double horse trailer. Molly was excited about the outing; especially so when she found out that Indian Summer was going to be her horse. Liz was a bibliophile and loved to talk books with Molly. Molly was curious about horses so they had an interesting friendship.

"Where are we going?' Molly asked as they turned off Hwy 151 and headed south on Rt. 45.

"Jersey Flats," answered Liz. Instantly Molly felt a warm glow that began in her tummy and then spread out all the way to her finger tips and her toes. Suddenly, the morning took on an air of destiny. Early morning clouds had been shooed away by the sun and the day was becoming bright and warm. The trees were now in full green foliage and everywhere there were birds.

Bim Stouffer was happy to see the sun come out to mellow his morning in the garage. Things had returned to normal following the departures of Ray Jr., Carrie, and Mike. Bim was happy in his own way that the kids had gotten hitched finally. He knew Pat was a little disappointed that she had been denied planning a wedding, but those late-in-life weddings he felt were needless and tedious. It was sensible to just go to the justice of the peace and get it over with. Pat knew it, too, deep down. This sensible thought allowed him to morally crack his first cold beer of the day.

Pat was gone for the morning doing some sort of charity work with her church women, which gave Bim the time and space to relax and enjoy the day undisturbed. The morning was filled with the sound of lawnmowers up and down the street, but he liked that sound. He might even mow himself later if he got the urge. Right now, though, was a time for quiet contemplation. He got up and walked to the back wall of the garage and reached behind an old rusted tool box and pulled out a book. It wasn't that he was ashamed of what he was reading; he just kept some things to himself. Like his old friendship with the author.

Bim was plodding through *The Needle's Eye* by his old drinking buddy, Roland Heinz. In the old days he and Roland had worked at the quarry together and then played together a little after work. Bim looked up to Roland, who was a few years ahead of him in age and light years ahead of him in life. Roland had a depth to him that Bim admired. He had learned a lot about the wider world from Roland's war stories and then later, his divorce stories. He had been something of a disciple of the great man in the years before he was anything but great. Since then, he was getting to know his old friend through his books. In the old days Roland had gotten him excited about things; now he calmed him down.

After a couple beers and a few pages of Roland's prose, Bim was transformed. He was able to rise above the streets of Fond du Lac and look down like a bird high in a tree. As if on cue, Bim's eye caught a flash of red motion and looked up from the book in his lap. A big male cardinal had crossed the driveway and lighted on top of the trellis which leaned against the house waiting for Pat's roses. The bird delivered a loud, *thweet-thweet, chew-chew-chew-chew*.

"Well, good morning to you, too. What are you up to?"

The bird hearing the voice flew away, but Bim heard very distinctly in his head an old familiar voice that answered his question: *About six-two!*

Bim got a chuckle out of that and went back to his reading.

There were a couple other horse trailers parked off the road at the Jersey Flats Prairie Development Project. Molly mostly looked on as Liz got the horses out of the trailer and saddled them. She instructed Molly as she went along so that she could do it herself the next time they went riding. Finally easing herself up onto Indian Summer, Molly was a little hesitant, but the horse sensed that and nodded patiently, waiting for Molly's intentions.

"He likes you, Molly," said Liz.

"I like him, too, but I hope he's okay with a new rider."

"He's very gentle. We'll just take it slow."

"Okay."

Liz clicked her tongue and prodded her mare slightly and Molly's horse followed the cue. They set off across the prairie grass sending mourning doves and grasshoppers flying away in front of them.

"Where we going, Liz?"

Liz pointed ahead to the mound of boulders and trees in the middle of the large field. "Let's head over to that kame."

The kame. There was that strange word again. Ever since the dream of Roland it had been stuck in her head; sometimes nearly forgotten. Now after driving past it a few times, she was on her way to actually visiting it. "*Find the kame,*" Roland had said. Now there it was, right between the horses ears and she was aimed right at it.

Owen saw the two horses approaching across the prairie and didn't think much of the intrusion into his morning solitude at first. He knew the prairie and the nearby trails were favorite destinations for riders in the area. More than once he had watched horses cavorting over at the ranch between where he sat and Dundee Mountain. He figured these two riders would go right on past without noticing him. Just in case he walked back into the trees to hide. He wasn't sure why he was doing that, but he felt it might have something to do with him looking ridiculous, sitting day after day alone on a hill. He sat down on the ground in the shade and closed his eyes. He waited about ten minutes until he was sure the riders had gone by and then walked back out to his perch. To his surprise, the two riders were stopped just down the hill in front of his perch. He could see now that they were both women and one of them was looking up the hill and straight at him. When she got off the horse and started walking toward him, he knew instantly who it was. The other rider, still astride her horse, waited and watched.

Molly was slightly breathless when she arrived at the top of the kame. It wasn't so much the climb as the fact her heart was racing wildly. She finally walked up to Owen and stood about five feet away. Before she spoke she looked around and took in the view.

"I've been looking for you." She said and after a long pause, "All of my life."

"Molly, I…"

"Don't talk. Let me say this, okay?" He nodded. "I heard your explanation of why you've been avoiding me and, okay, I respect your reasons. But god, Owen, don't I get any input into what is right or wrong for me?"

Owen shuffled his feet nervously. This whole thing was overwhelming him. He was trying to listen to Molly and figure out how she had found him at the same time. It was making his head spin.

She seemed to be reading his mind. "Okay, it looks like you and I have wandered into something weird," Molly said. "At this point I don't really care how all this happened, but here's how I see it. You lost your practice, which means you are going broke. You might have to move away, right?"

Owen nodded.

"Well, I have a solution to both our problems and I think you should consider it."

"You do?"

"I have a big empty barn on my property that would make a perfect location for an animal clinic. I have a studio that would make a wonderful guest house. I have a house full of women who need a man close by. I want you to move your practice to Pipe, Owen. There is a ready-made clientele in the area. The nearest animal clinic is Fond du Lac or Chilton. Most of all, I want you and I to get to know each other. We both know that something has been drawing us together ever since I brought that owl to you last March. Hell, look at us right now. What are we doing meeting on this...this freaking kame? And don't think for a second that I am stalking you. I've got witnesses." Molly pointed to Liz, who waved back.

"All of your plans would cost money. Lots of money. I sure don't have it."

"I do. My father, Roland left me loaded. I don't give a rat's patootie about money. Besides, I am not buying you. I have no doubt your practice will succeed and you will pay me and the girls back. Call it an investment."

"And what if things don't work out? With the practice or us?"

Molly stared off at Dundee Mountain. Her heart whispered to her brain a simple truth. "Everything...all of it is going to work, Owen. All you need to do is walk down from here and start packing. I have never been more sure of anything in my life. Getting you back to work is the first step. Anything that happens after that will come from that beginning."

"How can you be so sure?"

Molly looked at Owen's face and noticed that some of the reconstructive surgery was working. He was gorgeous with a tan. "Do you believe in ghosts?"

"Ghosts?"

"Yeah, dead folks who come in dreams and visions to enlighten the living."

"Maybe."

"You and I, Dr. Palmer, have been given to each other by a ghost. A ghost who wrote our story in his imagination and then came back here just long enough to make sure the story came true. This thing that you and I are about to begin was started when these boulders were moved down here during the last Ice Age. Sometimes good things take a long, long time. The glacier stopped right here." Molly toed the ground with her boot. Owen glanced around.

"I've gotta go back down and finish my ride. You come out to my place tonight for dinner. About six will be perfect. That sound okay?"

Owen nodded. "Six o'clock."

Molly turned and walked down the kame to where Indian Summer was waiting patiently for her. She climbed back up into the saddle and Owen watched as the two women veered off east toward the tree line. His first thought was that something amazing had just happened, but he wasn't sure exactly what it was. His second thought was that he needed to go home and start checking out the internet for a cheap moving company.

EPILOGUE

The man who sat in his garage was sleeping: chin down on his chest and hands folded in his lap over a closed book. His breathing was rhythmic and produced a soft snore. Seated on either side of him were a tall man and a wide woman. They were both enjoying a cold can of beer and the soft afternoon sunshine. The shade of the garage was cooling and quiet; as silent as eternity.

"Tomorrow's gonna be June already," said the woman.

"Yes, a fine month around here," the man added.

"I remember that."

"It's nice to come back home from time to time, isn't it girl?"

"Nice, yes, but it confuses me sometimes. Why are we here with this sleeping man in a garage, father?"

The man set down his beer can and put his hands behind his head. He leaned back in his chair and smiled a smile that was brighter than every sun in the universe.

"We come where we are invited. This man was an old friend of mine and he wanted to spend a little time with you and me today. He felt a certain pleasant peacefulness in his soul that made him want to take a little walk into our world."

"Is our world so different from his?"

"Not really. They parallel each other. The structure is different, but the images are the same."

"How so, Father?"

"You see this sleeping man, right?

"Yes."

"You see that he has a book in his lap, right?"

"Yes, I do."

"Well, girl, while we sit here and dream about him, he is sitting there dreaming about us. The magical connection is the book."

"You wrote that book. I see your face on the back cover."

"Look closer and you will see the face of every character and everyone who ever picked the book up and read it. You will see yourself. Look even closer and you will read every word ever written, every story ever told. Look closer still and read between the lines and you will find the place where the bards and poets sing like the birds of Heaven."

"Imagine, all of that in a book," the woman sighed.

"Yes, my dear, just imagine."

Some time later the man in the garage awoke from his nap. He was still holding the book in his lap with his finger keeping the place where he left off. He awoke just in time to see that the cardinal was back on the rose trellis. For a moment, in the confusion of his waking, he mistook Wisconsin for Heaven.

LaVergne, TN USA
09 September 2010
196538LV00001B/2/P